THE DAY OF THE COVERT REVELATION

THE DAY OF THE COVERT REVELATION

Brian Appleby

The Book Guild Ltd
Sussex, England

First published in Great Britain in 2003 by
The Book Guild Ltd,
25 High Street,
Lewes, East Sussex
BN7 2LU

Typesetting in Baskerville by
IML Typographers, Birkenhead, Merseyside

Printed in Great Britain by
Antony Rowe Ltd, Chippenham, Wiltshire

A catalogue record for this book is available from
The British Library.

ISBN 1 85776 760 8

PROLOGUE

Hi. My name is Linda. I'm 33 years old, and now married with two daughters.

Three years ago I was working as a freelance writer/journalist, earning my keep like everybody else, and living alone in my own world in south-west London. Then one spring day I stepped into another dimension – a world I couldn't believe could happen to me.

Within 24 hours, my life dramatically began to change. The next four weeks that followed, in which time period this book covers, had made me realise what life is really all about. Today, I do live in a fast-changing world for the better.

Read my exclusive story of adventure in those crucial short weeks that changed mankind. My 'odyssey' begins in early June 2001.

The complicated technicalities I have left out, but believe me they are there, even today, with back engineering, it is incomprehensible.

From the official version, I have adapted this book to keep my story as simple as possible, to read in the third person as it happened, just like Harry and myself experienced, the walk into the unknown. The privilege I have, after receiving permission, is to be able to relate this to you after being commissioned by the highest authority concerned.

Also I'd like you to bear in mind that four weeks is not long, considering the situation. The private and personal feelings between Harry and me are excelled by that very fact.

To put it bluntly, the life of a dog is seven to one in years compared to humans, and one month for us both is equivalent to seven months together.

PART ONE

GENESIS

1

Linda, a freelance writer, found an old news item about a missing adventurer, a Professor Daniel Kent. On reading, she found in the news item that this man was like the Indiana Jones type of adventurer. Linda was intrigued enough by the story for her to make a feature out of his disappearance for a magazine later in the year.

His disappearance many years ago in the sixties was investigated, but no trace of him was ever found. He was last heard of in the Avebury area of Wessex.

Linda in her research discovered that there was a son, a Harrison Kent, living in southern England, who was following in his father's footsteps, a Doctor of Geomorphology, a geographer.

For the feature, she had to get permission from him and hopefully an interview as well. Linda rang his home, and was informed by the housekeeper that he was away on a geological trip. In the conversation, she learned that his mother died ten years ago and his ex-wife left him five years after his mother's death.

Linda was asked to ring back at the end of the month, when he was due back, for an appointment. The housekeeper stated she was sure Mr Kent would be pleased to give an interview. Linda thought it was odd for a housekeeper to say that on his behalf. Meanwhile, on that presumption, Linda gathered as much information as possible on his life

3

and family and compiled a list of questions for the coming interview. In the meantime, the information she picked up on this missing man made her feel drawn to it. This story could be one of her best features to date, could even be the big one. There was not much on the son, which is understandable.

Linda phoned him a few days after his return from abroad, explaining her reasons for writing the feature, with his consent of course. He seemed interested and they made an appointment to meet at his house for the interview. He gave Linda directions to the house, which was hard to find, being at the end of a country lane.

JUNE

Tuesday

On the way down, Linda was thinking that he sounded nice on the phone and this was a good story and would help her very much. It was a make or break feeling for her. She hoped the interview would go well.

His directions told her to drive through the village, fork left at the garage, then drive for two miles until she saw two white posts at the beginning of a long lane. The house was at the end.

The house had a large driveway and she parked by the front door. At the drive entrance, Linda noticed the name *Anastasia* on the gate. It was a big house, at least four bedrooms, built in the thirties, well-maintained where necessary, but could have done with a lick of paint in places. A nice large garden starting on the left of the house, around to the west-facing rear. The view was stunning, with the sea miles away to the south between the Downs.

Linda was already picking up good vibrations of the man and the house. Was her intuition telling her right? She was very nervous, unusual for her. Her feelings were unexplainable.

She rang the bell.

The housekeeper answered the door. Her name was Delia, the lady Linda spoke to on the phone last month. She was about 50, and very attractive for her age. Delia looked as if she enjoyed life when she was young. She had been housekeeper here for 30 years, employed by Mr Kent's parents.

Linda was shown through the house, passing the front room to a large kitchen/diner facing the rear garden with a conservatory attached to the diner. Delia said Harry was in the garden cutting the grass. 'I'll tell him you are here.'

Linda looked out on to the garden, covered in shrubs and other plants. There must be over an acre of land here, not including the house, she thought. There was also a spinney of larger trees at the far end of the garden. The whole grounds would be a heaven for kids to play in.

Linda then saw Delia standing on the patio. looking down the garden. Then a man on a grass-cutting tractor appeared going around the shrubs with the grass as walkways between them. He disappeared now and then as he made his way around the grounds. He saw Delia waiting on the patio and he made his way up to her. He switched off the engine and Delia spoke to him. He dismounted the tractor and started to walk towards the house, talking to Delia.

Linda could now see for the first time the man she had come to interview ... she was not disappointed. He looked about 5 foot 10, no taller, also quite good-looking to her eyes. She also thought he could look after himself in most situations. About 35, with light brown hair, not thinning at all, and blue eyes. Not bad at all, she thought. Her fears were beginning to disappear, but other unexpected feelings were coming to the surface, she felt relaxed. This interview wouldn't be so customary as she had thought it would be. There had been a few dull ones in her career.

He came into the kitchen and greeted her with a nice natural smile and with a firm but gentle handshake.

'Sorry,' he said with feeling, 'I did not meet you personally. I have a lot of odd jobs to catch up on since I have been away, and you have to take advantage of the weather while it is dry. So much rain lately. Let's not be formal, please call me Harry. May I call you Linda?'

'Please do,' said Linda, charmed. She became immediately relaxed with his manner.

He showed her to the south-facing sitting room and they sat down at each end of the sofa, facing each other. Just then Delia came in with a tray of tea with home-made cakes and placed it on the small table in front of them, then left them to it.

Linda already felt at ease with him, but wanted to get the interview started. There was so much to ask. But somehow with his small talk – not the polite chat you normally get – she responded and realized there was really no rush at all.

He told her, he said, he'd just returned from the Far East a few days ago. Now, with extra leave he was home for the summer, then off to the States in September.

After an hour had gone by, with the pleasant talk, tea and cakes, Linda had to ask if she could now possibly start the interview.

Of course,' he said reluctantly. 'Let's go to my study, all my papers are there.'

He led the way to a room facing the side garden. Up to now, Linda had noticed the house was clean and tidy. But in the study, there were books, papers and magazines all over the place.

'Sorry about the mess,' he said. 'Delia is not allowed to touch anything in here, except to clean. I know where everything is. You might say I'm too lazy to file, always cross-checking.'

At that moment, Delia came to the door and said she

would be off to do the shopping later. 'Is there anything extra to add to the list you gave me earlier?'

'No, I don't think so at the moment,' he muttered, thinking. Then he went to a desk drawer and took out a credit card from a wallet and gave it to her, telling her it was a new one that needed signing.

'Lunch will be in a few minutes. Will Linda be staying?' enquired Delia.

He looked at Linda as if he was reading her mind. Linda started to say something, but he quickly said, 'Yes, Linda will be staying for lunch.'

Linda replied, 'Thank you,' but felt a bit awkward. The decision was taken out of her hands. Then she saw him smiling at her. Having given in, she smiled back and accepted the situation.

After a light lunch, Linda was thinking that time was passing fast and she did not want to be rude, but she still hadn't started the interview. The one thing she hated was rushing an interview. But somehow he was making her now feel flustered and she had to compose herself.

He looked at her and said, 'Look, let's go outside in the garden and do the interview there. It's a lovely day. I usually work in the study in the evenings. Shall we?' In saying so, he swung open the large French door to the garden, allowing Linda to pass through.

They sat at a table on the patio. While Linda prepared herself for the interview, Delia brought cold drinks out to them.

Suddenly, Linda was surprised by what he said next. He proposed that as the day was passing quickly and that it would be late afternoon by the time they finished, would she like to have dinner with him tonight?

Linda was tongue-tied. She composed herself again and started to speak. At last, she managed to get her words out, with the feeling all this was planned and the interview had purposely been delayed.

'I would love to,' she said, without thinking what she was saying. This was an important story to her, but she had to explain that it would make it late for her to return to London.

'I've thought of that,' he said. 'Stay in my guestroom over night and go home in the morning. Delia will look after you, as she lives in. That is, of course, if you don't have any objections or appointments tomorrow. If you are happy with that, I'll book a table at a country pub I know quite well, a few miles down the road.'

Linda did not, and was now pleased that she had been invited out. She was her own boss, and it was not very often she had the chance to mix business with pleasure. The thought of it gave her a nice warm feeling inside.

He then suggested that they move to the garden seat under the only large tree in the grounds of the house.

Linda got her act together and shyly asked the question, 'What if I was an ugly old maid that turned up to interview you – I would have gone by now!'

The answer he gave made her look up in surprise! Once again she had to compose herself. What is it with this man, making her accept what he says and comply with his wishes?

His reply was that he knew all about her stories in certain magazines and even newspapers. Her features were non-biased, fair and truthful. Also she made sure her facts were correct without twisting them around. She was a well-respected journalist. 'Besides,' he said, with a cheeky grin, 'your photograph always companies your features. So you see, I cheated. I knew what to expect … and took it from there.' Linda felt she was at a disadvantage. For a change, the interviewee knew more about her than she of him! She had to smile to herself.

The interview went on for nearly two hours, starting with Delia, the housekeeper, Anne, his ex-wife, then about his parents plus more detail on his father for most of the interview. Linda was enthralled by his father's adventures – something out of *Indiana Jones*, without the film dramas.

He was on his last quest when he had disappeared. Some of the details Linda did not understand, nor did his son for that matter. There was some paper work in the study about what his Dad was looking for, maps and reference books. But hardly any personal notes, most of the information he kept in his head. Harry understood the mission from the maps, but for what purpose, he was at a loss. He needed that one lead to understand, and he thought his Dad found it when he disappeared, so close to home.

It was only since his divorce that he decided to take on the task of his father's mysterious disappearance. No body, no reports or sightings. Harry was five years old when his father went missing. His father married at thirty, his mother – Angela – slightly younger. She died from cancer ten years ago. Thankfully, it was very quick – there was no cure. Harry married on the rebound. No children from the marriage. His ex-wife was his secretary when he was in the office. Now he'd been working in the field for the past nine years.

It was now late afternoon, the interview had to stop. Not only did they need the break, but also they were booked in at the pub for 7.30.

Linda was pleased she had her story. Sometimes a story flops. This one wouldn't. It was a good one. Could be her best yet! There were a few loose ends to clear up; maybe she would clarify those facts tonight. If not, tomorrow. Linda did not want to put the story to bed until she was completely happy with all the details.

They went on their date, had a nice meal and enjoyed themselves. They talked more on private matters not shop; she did not want to spoil the evening by bringing it up. All went well, and Linda did not feel deprived. She enjoyed his company, felt safe and trusted him.

Back at his home, Linda went to her room, which had an

en-suite bathroom that Delia had shown her earlier. Some nightclothes had been laid out for her in case she needed them.

Linda lay awake for hours, her head filled with all the facts. Her editor would be pleased with this one. She kept referring to her notes and finally her tapes. Then she had a silly thought – why on earth did it enter her head? Although she knew he would not try anything, she half-hoped . . . But Delia was in the house. Stupid bitch, she thought of herself, too soon, and with that she went to sleep.

Wednesday 13th

The next thing Linda knew was being woken by a knock on her door – it was Delia saying that breakfast was at eight and the time was now seven. Linda had a shower, then had a tidy-up and revised any last questions to ask before she returned home. Linda went down to the kitchen a few minutes early. Harry was already there and Delia was serving up bacon and eggs. She noticed that both of them looked tired. With a smile Delia asked if she enjoyed the evening? She did not hear them come back as she lived in a granny flat, two rooms converted on the north side of the house. Her evenings were always free, even when Harry was at home, except when there were dinner parties. Linda looked at Harry for some reason, then she realised what she was thinking – you did not come to me last night! With a hot flush she promptly forgot the embarrassing thought. What is the matter with me? she told herself. Three surprises in 24 hours are more than a girl can take! Then she realised why. Oh no! She said to herself I'm falling for him; I can't be in love! Surely?

Unnoticed, Delia was watching Linda and smiling, with her own private thoughts.

In conversation over breakfast, Linda said she needed to clarify certain facts. She was not now in any rush to get back home. Although Harry seemed to be in deep thought, he had a certain twinkle in his eye. 'OK,' he replied. 'We can go to the study and you can take a look at Dad's maps and papers, which you didn't see yesterday. Feel free to ask any questions. Anyway, I want to discuss something with you.'

Harry's thoughts had been obscure about women until this week – in having a divorce, which was a hard battle, and his mother dying young. He involved himself more in his work, which he enjoyed. Working with female colleagues, he was OK. but any advances by women made him back away. He classed himself as shy when it came to one-to-one relationships. Perhaps he was afraid or had not yet met the right one. His ex-wife made it a tough lesson to go by. When he returned home for the summer and Delia told him about a lady feature writer wanting to interview him about his father, he gave the matter some thought. His father was well-known in certain circles and it might help to solve the mystery of his disappearance. Linda rang at the weekend to see if she could see him about a feature she had in mind. He was interested. So they arranged a meeting.

He was impressed by her professional attitude and by her voice on the phone. He felt it was worth a try. He could always withdraw his permission. On this point, he told her so, and she accepted on that understanding. Anyway he felt something in his bones – time would tell. Her name rang a bell; he looked in his magazines, but to no avail, so he asked Delia if she had any magazines. There he found her in a popular woman's circulation paper. Then he remembered she did some short features in the national newspapers. He found what he was looking for, a photograph of her. He liked what he saw, then left it at that. Voice and photo only told one part of the story. At least he knew what she looked like. She had long auburn hair, her age was given as 31 and she was single.

The date on Delia's magazine was six months old. He felt a cold shiver as he realised that a string of coincidences had crept up on him. 'This paradox will go, take it as it comes.' He pondered on the thought as he went to see Delia about the shopping list she wanted, now that he was home for the duration. Delia was an attractive woman, very trustworthy and had long service with the family. When Harry's mother passed on, she worried that she might have to leave. She and Harry discussed the matter. Delia at 51 was very relieved that she could stay on in service. Harry needed someone to look after the house while he was away. Now that Harry was staying single, she provided what he needed. Besides, he was very fond of her. He gathered, that Dad was too, from the stories Delia told him when he was a boy.

Harry was cutting the grass when Linda arrived. He wanted to get it cut while the weather was fine. Although no time was given, Linda arrived earlier than expected. On seeing her, he was not disappointed. She looked better than the photograph. Her hair was cut shorter and complemented her features. She wore rings, but not on her wedding finger. He took that at face value. She was dressed in a lightweight trouser suit and looked very feminine. Harry tried to imagine her in other clothes, but his pulse started to rise. 'Control yourself,' he said to himself, 'it's only a woman to interview me.' One further look and then he got on with the business. She filled the suit very nicely.

After lunch, he rang the pub to check if he needed to book a table that evening. There was no need to book, but he still reserved a particular table he liked. He then had a word with Delia in the kitchen. She liked Linda, then said to him, 'Watch the body talk; she is all for you, and watch if it eases off or not. She doesn't know it, but she is giving herself away.'

In the interview, they got down to business, but he kept Delia's comments to hand.

The pub meal proved very enjoyable. Harry surprised himself; the conversation was relaxed, and with Linda he found this came naturally with her company; she was different from other women. He could not explain the reason why on the first evening together, perhaps the answer would come later. Maybe it was just down to two people out together? Harry needed time. He liked Linda's expressive face and he could read those eyes that talked to him. Harry would know if she ever lied to him. If he got to know her better later, he would be able to read her like a book.

Late that evening, Harry went to see Delia in her flat to talk. He often did this when he wanted to talk things over or just to seek her advice. He had lain awake thinking of Linda earlier. Delia did not mind the late hour at all; she was half expecting him anyway. They talked for over an hour. If only, Harry thought, Delia was younger ... anyway she was like a second mother to him. Then Delia came out with an unexpected surprise for Harry.

'I think it is time to let you into a big family secret,' she said seriously, almost coming to tears. Harry was taken aback, mystified by her words and emotion. Delia got up quickly and went to her bedroom, a few moments later returning with an attaché case and giving it to him apprehensively.

'I'm sorry,' she stated. 'Your mother gave me this for safe-keeping, shortly before she passed away, with strict instructions from your father to hand this over to you when I thought you are ready. I have abided by her wishes. I can't tell you how relieved I am to let you have this now, to watch you all these years looking for the right moment. There is no key, just the combination lock. Your mother or I do not know the combination, so you will have to force the case open. I do have some inkling of what is inside. If it weren't for the cancer your mother would be doing this now, she knew everything, but she took it all to the grave with her. I think you will understand now when you read your father's papers. Your father and I talked many an hour into the night, but he always held back certain facts, so I couldn't put it all together at that time. I now think differently as time and technology pass by. It is now thirty years!'

Harry was silent, taking in Delia's words. He felt that Delia was holding back something, she was not telling the whole truth for some reason. There was more to her than met the eye on this situation.

'Are you open for questions later?' he asked quietly. She looked down, avoiding his gaze. 'Yes.'

In the study, he did not have Linda on his mind this time, but he still did not sleep that night.

In the study that Wednesday morning Linda sensed tension in the air. Harry had gone quiet, he was looking at her, pondering. Something was wrong. Linda stood and returned his gaze. He was building up to something. In those passing moments, Linda sat down, facing him. But not for long, as Harry uttered the words, 'I don't want you to print your feature on Dad – at least not yet! We both agreed on that understanding.'

'What!' gasped Linda with surprised anger. 'This is the big story for me,' her voice rising, 'I've put in a lot of time and effort on the research to this feature, it's a good story.' Then realising she had agreed to the rule she quietly said, 'What do you mean – not yet?'

'If you promise,' replied Harry, 'to sit and not to interrupt and leave your tape off, I will explain as best as I can, what has happened since last night to bring this matter up. Then you can ask questions, but above all, I want to trust you. If you can prove that to me, and not think of me as some kind of nutcase, you will then have a bigger exclusive. But if you think it is rubbish, you will lose your story or what's left of it. I know your reputation, but it depends on your attitude and beliefs, which are very important to me at this moment in time.'

14

Linda stayed silent and pondered for a few seconds. 'OK, I've nothing to lose in hearing you out.'

'Let's sit out on the patio,' said Harry, 'We both need the air.'

They sat at the table, and Harry placed an attaché case he had brought out with him on the table. Delia followed out with a tray with tea and cups for three. Linda did not notice at first, until Delia sat with them. This is getting interesting, thought Linda. Delia served, and then Harry proceeded to explain to Linda about the attaché case he received late last night. Linda kept silent as promised, questions queuing up in her mind. After a couple of minutes of listening to Harry, she pulled her chair closer to the table, a force of habit when she used her notebook, or when a subject proved to be interesting. For the next half an hour, her eyes watched him closely. His talking was interrupted once, at Harry's request for Delia to bring him a packet of cigarettes from the study. Linda joined him. She spoke only once, when Delia was indoors.

'I'm still listening. If possible I would like to see these papers.' Linda was in a trance by what she was hearing. She wished she could use her tape, there was so much to take in with her notebook closed on the table. She looked at Delia as if to say, is this true? Delia gave nothing away concerning Harry's explanation.

Harry stopped talking, drained his third cup, then lit another cigarette and inhaled deeply. He looked at Linda, waited, then said, 'Well?'

Linda understood what she took in, but again, she did not understand everything. What a paradox! Finally words came to her, and she stated her thoughts. 'You believe your father is still alive, don't you?'

'Yes,' said Harry. 'Then ... now I don't know, it's possible.'

Linda stood up and started to walk slowly around the patio, deep in thought. She stopped, turned and faced

Harry. In a hesitant voice because of the extraordinary information she had just received, she did not wish to sound cynical, but said, 'I do believe you . . . I see now why you don't want me to publish this story. The world would be in chaos. You're lucky I'm like you and believe there is life out there . . . . What do we do now?'

'Do you realise,' said Harry, 'that you are the trigger to all this; this gave Delia the opportunity to hand over to me my father's papers. It's destiny, the time has come to find out about my father. I have to follow it through . . . Linda, are you with me?'

'Yes,' replied Linda without hesitation.

For the rest of the morning, Linda and Harry sat or strolled around the garden, Linda asking questions to get a clearer picture in her own mind, as she was prohibited to make any record of the new information that had come to light. Finally by lunchtime, Linda had managed to persuade Harry to let her publish the original story up to yesterday. This, at least would give her a feature to fall back on in the coming months, while in the meantime she could help Harry. He accepted that on the condition he read and had a copy of the transcript, plus approval, before giving her permission to print. He was going to give her the go-ahead anyway, but he wanted to see how determined she was to achieve this story, along with her sincerity. He made her work hard for it, all the time watching her lovely face express her feelings. He learned a lot about her that morning without Linda realising what he was up to.

At lunch Linda confided to Harry that she ought to return home to London, to write up her intended feature, to get it out of the way so as not to be biased with any further information that might come to light later. Her editor would want the original by next week, and then she would wait and see what came up in the near future. 'You can't keep the editor waiting,' she told Harry. 'I do have to earn a living, you know,' she said jokingly to him. 'I'll be back by the weekend, trust me please!'

'That will be all right by me,' responded Harry. He trusted her and knew he would be missing her company already in the short time he had known her. 'You have a job to do. In the meantime it will give me more time to study Dad's papers.'

Mid-afternoon, Linda prepared to go as she checked her bedroom to leave; Delia came to the door. Linda thought she was going to say goodbye. But instead, she came out with words that made Linda look intently into her eyes.

'I don't know if I should say this, but Harry likes you very much, and I think I'm correct in saying you feel the same. All I ask, is . . . don't hurt him.'

Linda gave herself away by saying, 'Yes I do.' She respected Delia, who was more than a housekeeper to Harry from what he had told of her in the interview. She guessed Delia had strong feelings for him – like a son to her.

Then Delia stated something that shook Linda.

'Please act normally while you are away. I stress this point, because there is nothing you can do about it. Please do not be afraid – you are now being watched! Or you very soon will be. I cannot say any more. Take heed of what I say. You have come into information that most people would not believe.' Linda felt rooted to the floor. All of a sudden she had the feeling of fear shiver down her spine.

'But, how . . . who,' stuttered Linda. Why was Delia of all people saying this?

Delia cut in with a smile. 'Don't worry about it, be normal. You'll be OK. Just making you aware of the situation, that's all.'

Linda was on a high with this story. What Delia just said brought her back down to earth and she was now confused. She started to ask why, when Delia over-talked her by saying, 'We will learn more at the weekend after Harry has studied his father's papers. Thirty years is a long time to hold secrets and I want to know as well.'

Linda was intelligent and had covered many stories as a reporter, and knew that unusual things do happen, police, the government, people of importance. Even in this case, it could happen to her. She looked at Delia, who knew more than she was letting on, a mysterious woman.

Linda thanked Delia for bringing the matter to her attention. Forewarned was forearmed, and she took it in 100 per cent.

Harry saw her off from the drive. He was missing her already.

'Take care,' he said on their parting. 'Give me a call later.'

Back at home that evening, Linda sorted out her notes, ready to type out. Time was pressing on and she wanted to ring Harry first. They were on the phone for two hours. By the time Linda finally put the phone down, it was late evening and she called it a day for any further work on her feature.

Thursday

Linda was up early. She'd had a restless night, thinking about her story; she normally slept quite well, but this story was incredible to believe in the light of the new information she had received. The original story was exceptional, and she would keep to that for the time being. Linda could not relax until she had put the story to bed. It's going to be a long day. It didn't help with Harry appearing in her thoughts every time she stopped typing. At long last, by the evening she had completed her feature and was exhausted. She realised she hadn't eaten all day, or done anything else for that matter. Men! she thought. She had never felt this way before. She put the washing machine on and went out to get a meal of fish and chips. Afterwards she felt better, and retired with a strong nightcap.

Friday

Linda woke up late; she had slept heavily, but she did have a good night's sleep. She lay in bed wondering what to do. She was ahead of schedule, and not due back to Harry's until tomorrow. Linda swore she had a dream of Harry looking down on her in her bed. For a second she wondered what it meant? After some shopping, she was at a loss what to do. There were some jobs, but she was not in the mood to do them. Linda wanted to be with Harry. Oh, to hell with it, she thought, I'll give him a call and see what he says about returning today.

Harry was pleased to hear from her, and especially about coming back earlier than planned. He also mentioned that Delia told him that she would ring this morning. Somehow, Linda was not surprised.

As she had been invited to stay for a few days, he reminded her to pack a few things and not to forget his copy of her feature. He would also book a table at the pub. The thought made Linda feel warm inside again. Normally in her life so far, women were like cats and men were dogs. But this certainty she had so early, she could not explain. She decided to change her attitude, and see what would happen in the following days. She had nothing to lose in finding out.

As Linda had decided to take a few days off, but mixing some work with pleasure, she would be less formal at Harry's home, so she packed light summer clothes and her light blue sleeveless dress for the pub date. That would please him.

Today she would wear a skirt and a lacy blouse to start with. She left home about one in the afternoon. The journey would take about an hour, depending on traffic. When she left it was a nice summer's day, but in the direction she was driving black clouds were forming. Ten minutes to the end of the drive, the rain fell so hard that it was bouncing off the road.

Linda rang Harry on her mobile to say she would be there in a few minutes. She arrived at the height of the storm and started to dash from the car to the porch of the front door and met Harry halfway with an umbrella. She still got wet, though. By the time she reached shelter, her lace blouse looked like she was in a wet T-shirt contest She was a little bit annoyed, but when she saw Harry looking at her like men do, she found she didn't mind.

She went and changed, then joined Harry in the sitting room and chatted about his father. He also showed Linda all the relevant papers he had.

In the evening, they went to the pub for their dinner date. The conversation varied on various subjects. He liked to hear her speak. She more or less gave him her life history. Harry felt his confidence building when he was in her company. Again, they did not talk shop.

They returned home about eleven. A light was on in the hall and a glow of light from Delia's sitting room. She had a visitor; a car Harry recognised was parked by her door. He continued along the drive, passed Delia's flat to a barn about 25 yards to the rear and to the right of the house. There were no doors on the barn; it was big enough to park three cars. He drew alongside Delia's car. A sensor light had already been triggered between the barn and the house as they strolled back past the conservatory door to the kitchen door. They went into the sitting room and Harry put on some light music. Linda sat down, and waited for his next move. Harry joined her on the sofa.

Linda smiled to herself. She had a strong personality, but

was quite happy to let the man lead and be positive in his actions to the woman. Linda had always put her point of view across if need be. She was told once that it was one of her faults – not ladylike. Since then she had been conscious of her behaviour with men. But Harry was the first man to break down her defences. With him, she found she was behaving quite naturally; Harry was slowly demolishing that wall she had built around herself over the years.

After a few seconds, he said to her, 'Would you like a night-cap?'

'Mmmm, yes please, a whisky and soda.'

Harry made Linda her drink, then switched the main light off, leaving the table lamp on, and then sat down beside her.

Oh, he is trying to be romantic, thought Linda. She knew that he had not been serious with a woman since his divorce. Linda never married. Mr Right never crossed her path – until now . . . and at 31, she had never felt broody.

Harry stretched out his legs, and put his arms along the top of the sofa – in a relaxed mood, he closed his eyes. For a few seconds, all was quiet as the CD changed tracks. He opened his eyes and saw Linda looking at him in thought. He slid his arm onto her shoulder and she instinctively rested her head on his and snuggled down to him. His hand started to caress her hair and neck. She was relaxed and liked what he was doing.

'Tomorrow,' he said softly, 'we will have to get down to business. Some important facts have come to light from Dad's papers.' She looked up to him to speak, but instead his lips started to kiss her cheeks, her nose, then her chin. She responded to him with a couple of short kisses. Harry then gave her one long passionate kiss on the lips. After a couple of minutes of smooching around, she had to come up for air. She was aroused and she could see that he was too. She had to do something, and said to him as nicely as possible, 'Harry,

21

do you mind that we don't go any further, I'm … not ready just yet … I'm sorry.'

'I understand,' he said frustrated. He paused and said genuinely, 'I don't want to rush it either. It's got to be at the right time, I'm sorry I rushed you.' Linda was relieved, she had the same feelings. They sat there, still cuddling for a few minutes, chatting until they both cooled down.

They heard Delia's friend's car start up and drive away. Delia came into the kitchen to clear up before retiring to bed.

After she had gone, they came out and went upstairs to their bedrooms. At her door he said, 'See you at eight for breakfast.'

He kissed her lightly on the lips. 'Goodnight Linda,' he whispered.

'Goodnight.'

Harry went back downstairs to pick up his copy of her feature to read in bed.

He was happy with her story; it was a very good feature and not a hint of the latest information was mentioned.

Linda enjoyed herself, she was glad she had returned early. There was more here than just a feature to produce.

Except for the last day of the curse, Linda was very happy.

Saturday

Next morning at breakfast Harry informed Linda that he had read the copy of her story, and was pleased she had kept to her word by not adding the new information to the planned original. He then asked her, 'When is the publishing date?'

Linda replied, 'At the moment, the editor tells me that he plans to print for the September edition.'

'That's OK then,' said Harry. 'Plenty of time, if necessary, to make any alterations.' He continued, 'The story coming about now – if you can publish? Could be an exclusive if viable, for the national papers. You could do all right out of this. You'll be in your element.'

'I'm keeping an open mind about this at the moment,' responded Linda. 'I want proof!'

'From today,' stated Harry, 'I have given this a lot of thought and I want you to record everything – use your tapes and notebook.'

'I've taken care of that,' replied Linda. 'There are extra tapes in my case. Oh, by the way, I tried to use my mobile earlier, to tell a friend that I can't make it today to meet her, completely slipped my mind. There's no signal, may I use your house phone?'

'Of course,' said Harry looking puzzled. He checked his. 'You're right, no signal. It's usually three to four bars here.' He went outside with his mobile, with Linda following. 'It's the same outside, maybe there is a power cut or fault. I'll try again later.'

Linda made her call, then rejoined Harry in the garden.

'What a wonderful view you have,' she said, looking towards the Downs. 'How far is the sea from here?'

'About twenty miles as the crow flies; you can see the horizon between the Downs on a good day. At night you can see the glow from the town on the other side of the Downs and the red lights on the TV transmitting aerial well to your left. In between it's a black void, with the occasional car head-lights in the distance.'

'It's really beautiful,' stated Linda. 'Nice and quiet, just the odd bird singing. Your dad had taste.'

'Dad liked the isolation, no close neighbours, with the village just two miles away.' Harry looked around, then at Linda. 'Talking of birds, listen.'

Linda listened. 'I can't hear anything.'

'That is unusual,' said Harry curiously.

'What's that?' asked Linda.

'The birds. They are not singing! It's non-stop chatter

around here, and I'm used to it. Sometimes the dawn chorus is like a brass band waking you up in the morning.'

Linda listened again. She was in the quiet countryside and all was normal. She had to admit it was quiet – even as a townie, you hear the birds.

Harry let it drop; he appeared unconcerned, and just put it down to nature. But he was sensitive to his surroundings and that was the second strange occurrence this morning.

Anyway, there was work to be done. They went to his study and sat facing each other across the desk. Harry took a book from a drawer. 'I did not properly study this until after you went home, it's a journal of Dad's life. A few personal references, otherwise just dates and places he went to, but it helps to make it a clearer picture of his life.'

Linda took out her tape and notebook.

'As you know,' continued Harry, 'Dad was born in 1935, and was called to do his National Service in the Royal Navy. He was lucky that he went to many places around the world. He saw many sights when on shore leave at the ports the Navy visited. That must have sown the seed for his future. After that he studied to be a geologist. All the dates and places are in this journal. If you want any dates you can look at it later. He made a few discoveries, also brought back a few artefacts. Dad seemed to have bordered on the edge in archaeological study, perhaps as a sideline interest. I know he had friends in that line of exploration.' Harry paused for a moment. 'Then he became interested in the Holy Grail. I don't quite know what he means here, but later on, I gather he was looking for the Holy Grail of life. He travelled to the sites of monasteries and temples, the Himalayas and other religious places of worship. Yet Delia tells me that Dad did not believe in God, but she added that he believed in a "Governor," as he personally put it, up there? Remember that this is the late 50s. In the 60s, he thought he was getting closer. His last entry in 1970 states that he thinks he has now found the answer. No further details after that. As I told you earlier, Dad is last heard of in the Avebury area, of all places!' At this point Harry reflected. 'I was five years old when Dad disappeared. Mum never spoke of him or his work afterwards. Mum withdrew when I often asked her. Delia told me a few details on the quiet, but that's all. Just to keep me happy, I suppose. The other night is the first time in many years that she spoke about Dad. I could never understand the secrecy of it all until Tuesday night.'

While Harry was talking, Linda sat silently with her tape on, taking notes.

'I can see Dad's fascination with it all. I've been to many places in my work; it gets into your blood. Places where not many people go – even today. Then they are just sightseers. There are maps here with crosses on, which, I believe, are places of importance to him. Dad is very vague with his remarks. I'm trying to read between the lines here.

'Here on this page, he is more elaborate with his writings. He says that some places he explored were so isolated that he came across people who were not of this world, that they had been watching him for some while. They even invited him to inspect their ship; they were very hospitable and friendly to him. He doesn't remember much about the ship afterwards. He had the feeling of being introduced and interviewed for some reason. Now, we have heard of these stories over the years, long after the event in most cases. But in those days the population did not hear much about these goings-on. A lot of it was withheld ... He also says here that he met them again much later, but he doesn't state when or where. What surprised me when I read this is that Mum is involved this time!

'Let's stop for now, Linda, it is nearly eleven. In the meantime, you'd better get out of that so-called skirt...'

'EXCUSE ME!' exclaimed Linda with surprised shock, 'WHY?

Harry found that he liked teasing her, and Linda was beginning to learn of his traits.

'We are going up a ladder in a few minutes,' he stated, 'to go into the old storeroom above the barn garage. The staircase is unsafe, so we have to use the ladder. I've been meaning to repair the stairs, but I haven't got around to do the work yet. I have got you a pair of overalls to wear. Of course, if you don't want to ... you can stay here ...' He was relying on her inquisitiveness and hoping for the adventurous spirit in her.

Charming, she thought. I wore this to look nice for you, now I have to wear overalls – not very flattering. He wants to know if I am willing to dirty my hands ...

Just then Delia came in with a tray of tea for them.

He certainly likes his tea, thought Linda, amused.

Delia, smiling, spoke to Linda, saying, I have left a clean pair of Harry's overalls on your bed for you.'

Harry has planned this, thought Linda. I'll have to keep my wits about me if he is going to be like this.

Then she said, 'Why are we going up into a dusty old attic room?'

'Dad's effects are stored there. I helped to put them up there when I was about ten. That's a long time ago.' Harry's statement that she had to go and climb a ladder did not please Linda. She wanted to help Harry so much, but she accepted it as part of the search for his father.

Harry's eyes were teasing her. She misinterpreted his smile, and said to him, 'You don't seem to be shocked by all this.'

'Don't misread me, please Linda. I am very concerned to know what happened to Dad. Maybe at last I will get to the truth of it all. What does bother me though is this alien life, is it true? Reading from his notes, he appears not to be concerned.'

Linda apologised for her remark.

*   *   *

26

Linda went upstairs to change. The overalls were on the bed, neatly folded. Linda took her skirt, stockings and top off. She slipped into the overalls and turned up the trouser legs and sleeves, then looked into the mirror. Oh no, I look like one of the Teletubbies. Oh well, it's only for a half an hour, I hope! She looked again at herself and adjusted the body zip to her cleavage line. That should put some femininity into it!

She went downstairs to meet Harry in the study.

'Hello, you look great,' said Harry grinning, trying to boost her confidence. He then went over to her and promptly pulled her zip up to her neck, and said to her nicely, 'With all those creepy crawlies up there, we don't want them going on a walkabout in prohibited places, do we.' He then gently kissed her on the lips, took her by the hand and went outside towards the barn.

Delia was there to give a helping hand. While waiting, she had taken her mobile out of her car to check to see if it needed charging - it was OK, but no signal. She asked Harry if there was anything wrong with the phone.

Harry had forgotten about the lack of signal. He was putting on his overalls from the boot of his car as he replied to Delia, 'There's nothing wrong with your phone, Delia. We are not receiving a signal in this area; I suspect a fault in their system. Now that you have reminded me, I'm going to check it out before I ring the phone company. Sorry ladies, I've a funny feeling there is something wrong here, just here, where we are, even the birds are still quiet.'

Harry picked up the ladder lying against the side of the barn and propped it up alongside the wooded steps leading to the storeroom, which had been converted from a hayloft many years ago.

'Right girls,' he said, taking Delia's phone, 'follow me.'

He started to walk towards the drive entrance, checking the mobile as he went, no signal. The further he got away from the house, he thought he might receive a signal. They went into the lane, and immediately the signal went to four bars.

'Look at that,' he said, showing them.

He went back into the drive; the signal had gone again. They walked to the south side of the gardens and checked there. The same thing happened again. No signal in the grounds, but in the field, on the other side of the fence, full strength showed on the mobile. They carried on down to the spinney at the end. No change, three bar signal in the trees, none in the garden. It was the same on the north side of the house back towards the barn garage.

'Well, that is strange, weird in fact. The house and grounds are in a dead zone, according to the readings, and so precise, right up to the boundary fences.'

'What does it mean, Harry, what's happening?' asked Linda, looking concerned with Delia standing close to her.

'I've no idea at all, I'm completely mystified! All I can say is that, I don't think the phone company is at fault, probably the weather, a freak of nature. If so it will pass. I'll check it again later.'

Harry thought personally that something strange, was going on. He kept it to himself: he did not want to unduly worry them.

Back at the barn they got on with the intended business in mind. Harry climbed the ladder and checked to see that it was safe for Linda to come up, with Delia standing by the bottom rung. Linda came up slowly and carefully. She reached the top and Harry took her hand to help her to stand on the small landing by the door. They entered the room.

Inside, it was dark. The only light came from a small hatch overlooking where the cars were parked in the barn. Harry anticipated this and had brought along two torches. Linda followed him inside; he handed a torch to her. She proceeded to explore behind him, shining her light here and there. The floor was covered with tea boxes, trunks, wooden chairs and various other objects, big and small – plus 20-odd years of dust and ... 'Oh Nooo!' she cried. She had walked into a curtain of cobwebs, I knew this would happen to me, she said to herself, half-cursing Harry at the same time as she wiped the cobwebs off her face. Then behind her right ear she heard the concerned voice of Harry saying, 'You all right?' She then gave Harry a rare, very expressive annoyed look he had not seen before. He had to smile how womanly she looked. Then Harry said teasingly, 'Keep close to me, there's a big spider over there.'

She fell for it and grabbed his left arm and hand with both her hands at the same time.

For the next half an hour they looked in boxes, cases and trunks. They didn't know what they were looking for, but they guessed they would when they did find it. In the end, it was just bits of equipment, a few artefacts, old clothes and various odd bits from the house.

Harry was sweating, but surprisingly no complaint from Linda. He expected she felt the same. Linda was more disappointed than anything else. A dead end!

Back at the landing, Linda had begun to descend the ladder with help from Harry. Delia, who had been cleaning her car out, now stood at the ladder.

'Did you find anything?'

'No I'm afraid not, it's just junk now,' replied Harry. 'I will have it cleared out later.'

Just then they all heard a bleeping sound.

'What's that?' asked Linda.

'I don't know,' said Harry. 'Have you a pager, Linda?'

'No, I haven't.'

Harry listened to trace the sound. 'The bleeping is coming from the storeroom.'

They returned to the room, where the bleeping got louder. Harry and Linda slowly traced the sound coming from one of the trunks they had previously checked. They looked at each other, puzzled. No one had been up here in years.

Harry raised the lid of the trunk and they both peered in.

With Linda looking over Harry's shoulder, eyes wide open, they saw, by the light of the torch, what appeared to be a floppy disc for a computer on top of some old clothing. The bleeps stopped.

'That wasn't there earlier,' said Harry, looking concerned. 'Too many strange happenings have occurred today to call this a coincidence.'

'I'm frightened, Harry, there is something not right with all this.' Linda was putting two and two together as well. 'If no one's been up here in donkey's years, then where did that come from? Nobody had computers then!'

'You are right there,' responded Harry. 'Anyway, let's return to the house and see what the downloading brings up on the computer.'

As they walked to the house, Harry showed Delia the disc and asked her for some cold drinks and then to join them in the study.

Linda, meanwhile, went to her room, changed her clothes and freshened up. She was relieved to get out of those unflattering overalls at last. Then she joined the others in the study.

Harry placed the disc into the computer to download, then they waited apprehensively.

All was quiet; the disc seemed to be a blank. They felt deprived, disappointed in fact.

Harry sat down. Linda came up behind him and placed her hands on his shoulders, then gently squeezed them reassuringly.

Then to their surprise, a voice came through the speakers; the words they heard made them look at each other in disbelief.

'The disc you have placed in your computer is a short-range communications device adapted for your computer, so that we can speak to each other live. Please bear with me and I will explain.'

'OH MY GOD!' gasped Delia, 'It's . . .'

The voice intervened to cut her short on saying anything further, on the matter in hand. 'That's right, Delia – Harry . . . I know you will be shocked . . . it is your father.'

2

Harry did not move or speak. Linda gripped his shoulders. She was a newcomer to the family, but could not believe the words she was hearing. A mixture of her professionalism and her relationship with Harry came together, but the overwhelming thumping of her heartstrings confirmed her real love for Harry. This realisation in those short seconds of gripping his shoulders cleared any doubts and thoughts she had in her mind of him – forever. Her eyes welled up for Harry and the return of his father. Harry pulled himself together; feeling Linda's concern through her hands gave him the support he needed.

Getting over the initial shock, he blurted out the words, 'DAD . . . Dad, is it really you?'

'Yes, it is, son . . . take it slow.'

There was a long pause. The emotions filled the air.

He then continued where he left off, 'I'm going to put the viewer on now, so you can see me.'

The viewer came to life with a live image on the screen.

Linda wanted to help Harry, so she said, and by sheer luck, mirrored Harry and Delia's thoughts. 'You only look about fifty-five.' After saying that, she felt embarrassed by the question.

'Thank you, Linda, that's what space travel does for your complexion, and I'm honoured to meet you at last, and I must say you are looking very nice.' Linda was taken aback.

He knows my name! A charmer too, like father like son ...
And he did go into space after all with them.

Harry looked at Linda as if he was confirming her
thoughts, he then put his arm around her hips while still
sitting. Linda responded by placing her arm around his
shoulder and they both then cuddled each other. After a few
seconds, Harry stood up to speak.

'What's going on, Dad? What is happening? You have been
missing for thirty years ... WHERE THE HELL ARE YOU?'

'I will be making my way to the garden, meet me there in a
few minutes.'

This reply made them all look at each other in amazement
... here ... so close!

Like children they quickly made their way to the garden.
Once there, they eagerly looked out from the patio. Then
they saw someone sitting on the garden seat, partly hidden by
the islands of shrubs midway to the spinney.

Harry walked slowly towards him. Linda and Delia stayed
and watched this bizarre reunion from the patio. The man got
up and came towards Harry. They met, then a pause, then
they embraced each other. They strolled towards the spinney,
talking as they went. On reaching the trees, they turned
around and started to return through the garden towards the
house, stopping now and then. facing each other in deep conversation. At one point Linda saw Harry look intently up into
the sky, shielding his eyes from the sun. As they neared the
house, she noticed that Harry was slightly taller.

Linda sat and watched the two men. She was on the verge
of tears.

The two men came onto the patio. Harry's father kissed
Delia on her cheek and said something to her as he gave her
a brief but warm embrace. He turned to Linda, and waited
for Harry to introduce him formally. He took her hand
gently and also kissed her on the cheek.

'I have been longing to meet you, there is so much to tell

you – and thanks for being by Harry's side in his time of need. As you know, my name is Dan.'

Linda had the strange feeling he knew all about her. The butterflies in her stomach were beginning to raise their wings – this always happened when Linda was uncertain of something.

Harry asked Dad if he would like to eat.

'What a good idea – yes, I would like to have lunch. You can't beat food and conversation. Also I would like Delia to join us.'

Within a half an hour, Delia had prepared lunch while in conversation with Dan. This gave Harry a chance to bring Linda up to date. She switched on her tape, no notebook, as she was not sure of his father's reaction. They sat in the sitting room, and for ten minutes Linda kept silent; as before, she would ask questions later.

She was told that Dan had been watching him since he was a child, whenever he had the chance, also Dan had been here since early morning, observing, especially Linda. She knew it, her stomach doesn't lie. Mum's death was unexpected. He was away at the time, had he known he could have saved her. The cancer came so quick. Dan said he would give more details on this later.

'Dad – like in *Star Trek* – beamed in the disc we found in the storeroom.' Linda eyes widened slightly on hearing this, but she just nodded to say she understood. Harry continued. 'This was the only way he could make contact, without too much shock involved to me and to be in company with someone he could trust. Dad did not want me to be alone on first contact. But not Delia, he wanted someone from outside. He then chose you!' Linda's eyebrows rose higher, but this wasn't the time to start interrupting. It was all on tape.

'The problem with the mobiles is that they were neutralised, because of a force field around the house. This part will surprise you Linda. His "transport" is hovering above the

34

house in a fixed position, and it is invisible! At the moment, it is monitoring the force field and the surrounding area. The birds can see the phenomenon and just fly around it. They are not in any way harmed. This has answered some of the unexplained happenings so far today. Dad is here by himself and the precautions are for his protection. The protective ring around us recognises the DNA and the genetics macrocosm of the people permitted here and has many functions for various purposes. So you are free to leave if you wish to. If the postman turned up, he would deliver the mail, as normal, but Dad would know – to put it simply. Dad has been waiting for the right opportunity to make himself known to us over the past few days. That's all for the time being, and I expect there is a lot more to come.'

Linda took a deep breath and smiled. But her hands were shaking. She wondered if she was out of her depth here. Then her professionalism clicked in.

'Looks like I'd better put in a new tape and batteries for my recorder for lunch. Let's see if it is ready, I'm famished!'

Harry leaned forward and gave her a gentle 'thank you for being here' kiss on her lips.

The four settled down at the table in the kitchen/diner. Except for small odd bits of chat the meal was mainly eaten in silence.

Harry decided to get Dad to open up after Delia served up refreshments. He said, 'Dad there are so many questions. I think it would be for the best if you just tell us your story and we ask questions as we go along. What do you think?'

'Good idea,' replied Dan. 'Now where do I start?' He thought for a few moments.

'I think I will have to tell you in three parts. I'll try to keep it short and simple as possible. The first about me, the second part the technology, and last of all why and the reasons – the purpose that I'm back.'

He took a long look at Linda. Then he spoke to her directly, confirming he knew more about her than she realised.

'You may use your tape and notebook, Linda, I know all about the features you are writing. Bear with me, I will explain in time.'

The room was silent for a few moments; Linda wasn't quick enough to bring out the appropriate words in time to ask a question. It was all going over the top of her head at the moment. Anyway she had the tape running. She said to herself, come on girl, keep your wits about you, otherwise you're going to make hard work out of this! She must have shown some concern, because Harry placed his hand on her knee and said, reassuring her, 'Don't worry, I will help you as much as I can.' With that, she felt better. Harry needed her support, now he is for her!

After this short pause, Dan continued.

'When I started travelling and exploring, I soon found that my quest was for the "Holy Grail of Life". When I met the aliens, I was petrified. Luckily, they were friendly, because there is more than one race, and one is not friendly. They informed me that they had been observing me for some while. They knew all about me!

'Whom I met were scouts for another race, who were like us – humans. They took me with them in their ship; I tell you I was very apprehensive and scared to begin with! Was I being abducted? I was 30 years old then; although interested, I was also naïve. You only heard the odd story in those days. Anyway, a few minutes later, as I recall, I could see the Earth – oh, what a beautiful world Earth looked from up there.

'The United States were then trying to get man to the Moon at that time, and here I was looking down at Earth in 1965! The first man to land on the Moon did not arrive until 1969.

'The sphere we were in went into a bigger ship - a mother-ship which is in orbit around the Earth, and is still up there today! I then could see the mothership as we approached the docking area. I was informed that you couldn't see her until you are inside the protective shields of the ship. There I saw various forms of life from different worlds in the galaxy. The experience was very disconcerting at the time. Most looked like humans, others had variations. I sort of expected more contrasting differences. Then I was introduced to a man, similar to me, who is in charge and still is, which he called "The Earth Project". He showed me around the ship. He and I asked many questions. In the end he offered a proposal to me. Would I like to join them to help to improve Earth's survival in the coming years. If so they would train me. I said, I would have to think about it. I was very confused at the time: I'm trying to keep it short and simple in telling you because it's another story all together up there.

'Surprisingly I was returned to Earth. Think it over, I was told, we will contact you.

'So far I have told you the full facts, but at that time I could only remember part of the experience, it felt like a dream. I could not get my head around it, but most of the jigsaw came together over the next six months or so. But inside me the seed was sown.

'I came back to England. As my wife of two years, Angela, was pregnant. I decided to become a lecturer at universities and became a professor. Then I bought this house. It was at my lectures that I met Delia. She introduced herself by asking many questions. I will always remember that of you,' looking at Delia. 'Then we became friends. Harry was born, then we found that Angela suffered from severe PND for a year. So I started to look for a nanny to help out for the duration. Delia offered her services to help her finances through university. You were about eighteen, I think, Delia,' looking at her, she nodded in agreement. 'Angela and Delia got on

37

well, and Delia found her true vocation in service to my family and also became a part-time secretary to me in my work.' He paused here to gather his thoughts.

'Eventually, I confided with Mum,' looking at Harry, 'about my experiences two years previously. I was hungry for more information after the jigsaw came together about their mission. They said they would contact me, they gave no time period. But no word came, I did wonder at times if it were a dream. Mum thought I had, when I suffered from heat stroke at that time. I was worried about my sanity.

'Then one day, I don't recollect the date, two men arrived at this house. One of them I recognised as the man in charge of the Earth Project on the mothership, he is known as "The Master", to me he is Voss and we became friends. I introduced Mum to them. She understood all the facts but somehow did not believe them. She was very sceptical. She was one of those people who, if they don't see it in black and white, won't accept the truth. In this case, it was understandable. Gradually her attitude changed after many more questions, she said, "Prove it to me"! This they did by inviting us to the mothership. I could not understand how Mum had not been frightened. I saw her in a different light after that, a very brave intelligent woman! We went, and the experience was about the same, as I described earlier. The trip was much clearer this time, for some reason. Angela had always supported me in my work, ambitions and the quest that dominated my life.

'I was invited to join them, and Angela was welcome to join me. But in the end, she declined the offer because of you, Harry. Maybe when you were older. Mum wanted me to go with them to see if I could accept that kind of life. At least I was able to talk of my experiences to her on my visits home.'

Dan was grinning at Linda and Harry, and told them, 'I'm afraid I did not go missing at Avebury, although I did check the place out. The day I went missing was from here. Mum put the story out that I was at Avebury at that time. Just a slight cover-up.

'Delia had joined us in service permanently about a year earlier. In fact, she somehow found out about our secret and wanted to join the club. This was approved and consequently she became an operative like me. Delia's duty was as before, but in the knowledge about me, and the extra security that is required, and later, to wait for my return. That wait became many years. Delia must have thought I had died. She carried on with her duties and kept the secret quiet because of Harry and hoped that one day the truth would come out. That is now happening,'

Now Linda understood Delia's words and why she said them. She was trying to prepare me.

Although Harry had been in the dark about all this until now, he found he was not at all surprised. Dad must have had help in those early days, and besides Mum, Delia was the only one who lived in the house throughout that time and after, with this knowledge. Delia must have had one eye on the sky, and wondered if she would ever hear from them again. Her loyalty paid off. All that morning, Harry had noticed that Delia was very quiet, not her usual bubbly self. She must have guessed.

Linda also came to the conclusion that Delia knew more than she had let on, from the comments she said to her on the day Linda returned home. If Dan had not appeared, Harry and Linda would not have been at all suspicious and the story, without evidence, would have died a natural death ... unless Delia broke her oath ...

Linda changed her tape. The story was getting deeper and more interesting than she had expected. Nobody came up with any questions; they were waiting to hear the conclusion. Then Dan would have been bombarded by them.

Just then a low bleeping was heard. Dan then pulled up his right sleeve to reveal a small flush device on his lower arm.

He then touched the screen with his finger and he looked as if he was listening to something, but to the others in the room, all was quiet. Then Dan said, 'There is a car approaching the house from the road; as the lane is private, the car must be coming here.'

'Oh,' said Delia, 'I had forgotten about them, it's Pat and Helen coming up for tea. I invited them earlier.'

'No problem,' replied Dan, 'just carry on as normal with your arrangements, I'll see you tonight.' Delia left to meet them. Dan got up from the dining table and went to the front sitting room. Harry and Linda followed.

At the bay window, Dan could see the car arrive and drive around to the side of Delia's flat. Delia met them at her door. But they were out of sight from Dan's view. Harry came and stood by his side. Dan spoke to the device: 'Report:' he said distinctly. On the screen of the device, Harry saw the words, 'TWO FEMALES, HUMAN: ONE ANIMAL, BREED – DOG'. But Dan wasn't looking at the words; he was listening to the female's voice and looking through the window. This time Linda was by their side, now also hearing the voice. Dan spoke again. 'PERMISSION GRANTED'. He then gave another instruction, 'Anastasia'.

Harry asked 'What is the "Anastasia" order for? It is the name of the house.'

'Had I made a mistake, and they were hostile, that code word order would have activated. That command would have immobilised them.'

Then Dan continued, 'This is my personal communicator via my ship and the mothership. Also with this I can control my ship's functions when I am not on board – like now. No one can use this; it is activated by my voice only. I'm informed via my earphone; you can't see it. That part is implanted into the middle ear by injection and it is permanently there while on active duty. Thirty years ago or more, people would have looked at this in wonder. Today, neither of you batted an eyelid. Time and technology have changed things. This is one of the reasons why I'm here now. It was only in the 60s that the printed circuit came into being. Then followed the chip. Now look what you have.' They returned to the kitchen, to clear away the dishes. Harry took Linda's hand into his and asked how she was feeling.

'OK,' replied Linda, 'Except, I can't get over the fact that there is an UFO sitting above us and those two women don't know a thing!'

'Well,' responded Harry, 'I can understand Dad's quest for life. He certainly got what he wanted. He beats *Indiana Jones* hands down. What an adventure, and for thirty years as well. Excuse the pun, but it is out of this world. I wonder in what capacity he is here for?'

Linda pondered on that point; the butterflies in her stomach were beginning to fly.

After the break, they returned to the sitting room to hear the rest of Dan's story. Linda changed her tape around in preparation. There was one big question she wanted to ask. It could turn out to be a silly question to many people, but she felt it was an important point to bring up. It might clarify the situation and hopefully be more understandable; depending in which direction the question was answered. The reply she received was not the answer Linda visualised!

'Dan,' getting his attention as they settled down and before he commenced talking. 'There is one question I would like to put across to you before you proceed, if I may.'

Linda felt awkward and hesitated before she asked the question. He stayed silent and waited, observing her. Had he, and the computers, done their selecting correctly?

'Dan, these people whom you are with, do they have … a God … a belief, or a doctrine of sorts? I'm sorry, I don't know if the question is valid. I had to ask.'

'Do you have any questions, Harry?' enquired Dan, looking at him before proceeding to answer.

'I do,' answered Harry, 'but they can wait. Linda is the reporter. I'm leaving the ball in her court for the time being.'

Dan sat up straight and looked Linda in the eye. He respected the resolution put over by her, to be asked that question. He has chosen the right girl, hopefully in every way...

'You just hit the one million pound mother of all questions,' replied Dan seriously. 'I'm glad you brought this controversial subject to the fore.'

Harry, sensing the tension rising, interrupted and said jokingly, 'Do you want to ring a friend?' They all laughed. This put Linda at ease from feeling silly. Her enquiry now felt justified. 'No, I am able to answer this question myself,' stated Dan ... 'and that other one Linda wants to ask, about herself.' Both of them knew as their eyes met briefly. 'It is partly to do with my quest at the time. Both of you will be shocked and surprised, as I was, on hearing what I am about to say.'

Linda checked her tape footage. The next moment, she jumped on hearing Dan speak to her in a louder voice.

'LINDA! I will answer your question in a few moments. Sorry, but I have to say this first. YOU WERE PLANNED, you are principally the main character to this scenario.'

Linda, eyes wide open, was taken aback by this shock statement. Keep quiet, she thought, let him carry on; her stomach was turning over by her butterflies being suddenly jolted by these surprising words. Oh God, now what is he going to say!

Dan carried on. 'To plan this operation, we ... I needed a third person – down here ... and I found you, with the help of the resources from the mothership. I'm sorry, you were the right candidate, if I may use that, for the lack of the right word.' He waited a few seconds for the words to sink in.

'A few weeks ago, we induced into you the idea of a story

42

about me for a feature, and you took up the story. We needed a female writer for this operation. After a long search, we found you. I stress the point that we did nothing more than that. You went for the interview with Harry, after that we let nature take its course. We just observed from then on. We knew Harry would not turn down a pretty girl like you, Linda, on his doorstep looking for a story. Men are animals, aren't they, Linda?'

Linda didn't answer; she knew what he meant. 'We were 95 per cent sure we would be successful, anyway we kept our fingers crossed. So far it is working.'

Harry and Linda had similar thoughts. Yes, we are doing fine. I hope this doesn't alter matters.

'Now Linda,' said Dan, getting serious, 'this is your point of no return. If you now wish to withdraw, you will be free to do so, without any animosity, to leave. But I'm afraid to say there would be one stipulation. Your memory over the last few days will be erased by the time you arrive home. You'll think you are writing a feature for a magazine, you might print, who knows. But we want to commission you to write a book of your experiences, your point of view from the day you met Harry. We will tell you when to stop. You are doing well so far. I will tell you now, that there will be times when you will be under pressure, including stressful situations.'

Then Dan gave a short pause, to let Linda take it all in, and then said gently to her, 'Well, what do you say? Will you accept the commission and work for us?' Linda looked at Harry for some kind of reassurance. He smiled and nodded positively.

'I said yes to Harry earlier, and I will now say yes to you. How can a girl in my profession turn down an offer like that. Besides, I'm very intrigued.'

'Good, I'm very pleased you accepted. Now that is out of the way, I can get on with my account.' He could not proceed any further with her until he was sure of Linda's loyalty and commitment. Dan studied them for a moment before proceeding. He wondered how they were going to take it. Harry and Linda were now very apprehensive.

'This race of people I'm with do have a God, the same God. This race are the original civilisation from intelligent life, they were given a free hand in evolution and to populate the galaxy. Our Bible, which most of us don't understand, is like a child's ABC book of learning in comparison to their Bible. It is unprecedented, but if ever you do read it, you would see the light and understand their meaning of life.'

Dan paused again. 'The vastness of the Universe is beyond comprehension, let alone our own galaxy, and to top it all, our own human intelligent life, they put everything here on Earth! Over ten thousand years ago, when the Ice Age was receding. Before then, it was just animals and birds with other species of humans and themselves. A paradise! Of course, they had their own settlements on Earth, a very long time before thinking of putting human evolution of life here. When they did, it was a matter of time before civilisation and cultures came together to trade around five thousand years ago.'

Dan had to stop because Linda broke her pencil on her note pad. Recording this down all afternoon and trying to take it all in at the same time had become too much for her. She got up quickly and started to pace around the room, her eyes filling up.

Harry, still absorbing the narration, saw Linda getting into a state, rushed to her aid. Realising she was beginning to get hysterical, he immediately took her to the kitchen, then led her out into the garden for fresh air. Linda turned and buried her face into his chest, his hands rubbing her back and stroking the hair of her head, trying to comfort her.

Dan followed them out, apologising. He did not mean to be so forthright in his manner.

'Time for a break, I think, Dad!' said Harry insistently.

Trying to compose herself, Linda turned to confront Dan, and said in a half-shouted sobbing cry, 'And what do you call this so-called race! Not the *Atlanteans*, please.'

'Yes,' replied Dan, 'I'm afraid so!'

Linda's eyes rolled up, her knees gave way, and she fainted on the grass.

PART TWO

ILLUMINATION

3

Harry carried Linda to her bedroom; she was lighter than he had thought. Or it could be the adrenaline of the moment. He laid her on the bed and studied her face thinking how lovely she was and how lucky he was to have met her. Her breathing was normal, the windows were open and the room was cool. He made sure her head was comfortable on a low pillow.

Delia and Dan came into the bedroom.

'How is she?' enquired Delia, slightly out of breath.

'She is coming round slowly, she had me going there for a while.'

Delia looked at Dan and Harry and stated, 'Look at her, the poor girl. She is exhausted. You have been at it all afternoon. Don't you two realise what time it is; it's nearly seven. My friends went ages ago!'

They both looked at their watches, realising that time had flown by.

'Sorry,' said Dan, 'We didn't realise how late it is. If Linda is up to it later, then we will continue tomorrow – if Harry is agreeable?'

Linda opened her eyes and took a second or two to get her bearings. She saw faces looking down at her and was very embarrassed.

'I'll bring you up a cup of tea,' said Delia.

'Thank you.'

Then Delia stated on her way out, 'Dinner is at eight. Let me know if Linda is joining us?'

Dan and Delia left together.

Harry was still holding Linda's hand. She squeezed his, and then brought herself up higher on the bed and he helped her by placing a pillow behind her head.

'Thanks,' she said, then asked, 'what the hell happened? I can't get my thoughts together at the moment.'

'You fainted. It has been a long hot day and you got a little excited. We didn't realise how late it was.' He moved up and sat with her on the bed and gave her a reassuring cuddle.

Delia came in with a cup of tea. 'Everything all right?' she asked.

'Fine, thank you,' replied Linda.

'Good, it has been a stressful day for you.' She smiled and looked at Harry, who seemed to be taking it in his stride so far. 'Dinner won't be long.'

When Delia had left, Linda said, 'I'm getting my thoughts together now.' She paused, then in a louder voice in her defence, and poking her finger into Harry's chest stated, 'How can you say I was a little excited? How am I going to write this book I've been commissioned to do and put it into context, when I keep getting mind-blowing information that will shock us and cause chaos against our own civilised beliefs, UFO's, religion, our evolution and God knows what else! And it is just us two so far for starters.' Harry looked down at her finger that was practically embedded in his chest, then at her.

'Oh ... sorry, Harry, I ... didn't mean to ...' The look she got from Harry made her go submissive to him. She thought to herself, why is this man making me look up to him? No man has done this to me before. Then it dawned on her that it was her pride that had been dented, not her previous independence from a male-dominated society. Her love for

50

him was beginning to grip her heart in a vice-hold so strong she could not release it.

Harry's reply made her eyebrows rise and tighten her lips. 'Are you like this in the office?'

'What am I going to do, Harry?' she asked, then did the girlie bit by snuggling up to him for comfort.

'Well for a start, don't get so fired up like you just did, because that look in your face doesn't turn me on. Barring that, just relax and try to take things as they come. Keep an open mind; you've got to do that. The initial main shock is over now, just accept it from now on. That's how I'm coping with this situation, with the return of Dad, you and what he has brought with him – quite a scenario!'

Linda lay in his arms, deep in thought. I wonder what does turn him on?

'Oh, by the way,' said Harry, happily, 'I'm glad you accepted the commission, I would have been lost without you!'

'Lost!' she said. 'The thought of a blank memory after Tuesday is unbearable to think of: I would be at home now, doing the washing, bored out of my mind! And you drinking your tea alone.'

'Want me to bring your meal up to you?' he asked Linda.

'No, I'll come down, I'm feeling fine, now that we've cleared the air.'

They both lay together on the bed, now relaxed, laughing and sharing a cigarette, until about ten to eight. Then made their way down to the smell of dinner. Except for small talk, the meal went quickly, the subject matter dropped for the evening. Although the day had been long, Linda said, taking Harry's advice, that she would like to continue the next morning.

Dan went to Delia's flat for the evening. Harry and Linda took a late stroll around the garden. Linda looked above the house; she didn't expect to see anything: all was normal, just a clear sky. She then watched the last birds of the day. One or two that did fly towards the house did bank away as if there was something there, only because she knew, otherwise nothing out of the ordinary to anybody else.

They retired to the sitting room. Linda cuddled up to Harry on the sofa. She was happy and surprisingly relaxed. Today had felt, on reflecting, as if they gone through a 48-hour day, not 24. The morning seemed to be a haze on the distant horizon. There would be further surprises, as Dan had stated. But, as Harry said, the worse is over, the first shock is stressing. Now with better understanding and the knowledge, compared with the days leading up to this morning; there would be a lot to learn. They both realised that there might not be much time for each other. This is a fine romance, she thought, then she laughed to herself, I'm not mixing business with pleasure again . . .

As they sat there, discussing their thoughts, they looked at each other, Linda's eyes seemed to be talking to him. Harry was about to say something, but he paused, he could not read her face, then pushing his luck, he said, 'If we are going to cuddle here, and we are both tired – let's go to bed and cuddle there . . .'

Well, she thought, mildly shocked, that's a new one on me. She turned in her seat to face him, and gave him a short sharp slap across his face.

'That's for the proposition! she said, giggling. 'All right, but no funny business!'

Later, Linda surrendered willingly to Harry's charm. Her night of 'No funny business' turned into a learning curve of passion for both of them.

Sunday

Next morning, after a heavy sleep, they awoke to find themselves entwined in a tight embrace with each other. Because they both had pins and needles, they slowly had to untangle limbs. They started to laugh at the situation, then Linda fell out of bed with cramp in the thigh. Hopping around the bedroom naked, she had to go to the bathroom to get away from Harry's laughing. Later, he joined her in the shower to massage and soothe her pain away.

At breakfast, they helped themselves. Delia wasn't there. A couple of minutes later Delia came rushing in, looking slightly flushed.

'Oh,' she said, 'you have helped yourselves, I can do you bacon and eggs if you like?'

'We're fine,' said Harry, looking at Delia with a grin on his face. 'Where's Dad?'

'He is around somewhere,' said Delia.

'We will be in the garden if he wants us'

They sat at the patio table, Harry reading yesterday's paper as Linda checked her notes. Then they heard that bleep bleeping sound again. Dan materialised a few feet away from them. Both of them were startled at first. 'Sorry to make you two jump,' said Dan, smiling, 'I've just been up there,' pointing up, above the house.

'I take it that's how you get up and down, by transporting yourself – like in *Star Trek*?' enquired Harry.

'Very similar,' said Dan. 'They are not far from some of the truth in that programme.'

'I have to try that out sometime, to experience how it feels,' hinted Harry.

'If you like, you two can try it out later, no problem,' stated Dan.

Oh no, thought Linda, here we go again, got to keep face with the boys. I'll change into trousers later, just in case!

'Fancy a try, Linda?' asked Harry.

'I'll see, I'm not that keen,' said Linda reluctantly, knowing she would have to accompany Harry.

Dan had seen Linda's slight embarrassment. He expected

her to be cautious: just give her time, and then she will find that there is nothing to worry about. He then said 'I'll see you both in the sitting room about ten, OK?'

'Fine by us,' said Harry. 'Will Delia be there?'

'Yes, it will bring her up to date.'

An hour later, they were all waiting for Dan to start. With her new tape, Linda sat wondering what would be revealed today.

Dan studied Linda's face. 'You OK, Linda? Any problems, please stop me.' Linda nodded that she understood. 'Right, let's get started, we don't want another long day. It's Sunday, and nobody is expected. As I said yesterday, there were no humans on Earth. There were life forms similar to us, but not *Homo sapiens*. They eventually died out. When I say "they" from now, I refer to the race I'm working with. They put themselves on Earth to colonise it. They were all volunteers at the beginning, in the knowledge that eventually they would be left to their own evolution and civilisation. It was reasonably safe here, and for hundreds of years all went well. There wasn't any contact with this race and the people they put on Earth. They were left to fend for themselves. Memories faded in time with myths and legends. The rest is history. All this entire race did after that is to watch and observe like the rest of all the other worlds they populated.

'Their world is called Anthena. It is here that the first intelligent life is born, and it is from there they went forth to populate this half of the galaxy. The other side is not explored yet, but they are expanding quite fast now. To put it simply, there is on average one Earth world to each star constellation. At this moment in time, there are about sixty Earth-type planets in various stages of evolution. Some are well advanced, others are not. We are about a third or more up the scale of advancement in comparison with the others. All these worlds are many, many light years apart, so with advancement of technology, they will eventually discover each other. Earth has not reached that stage yet.

'One of their worlds they populated, I have to say, did not come up to their expectation, through neglect on their part and failing to keep observation on the evolution on this planet. They are now very hostile, and this has brought on a cold war between them, which has gone on for thousands of years.

'This world is called Nacania.

'Our Earth is one of their few favourites, and for a while, like I said earlier, they did set up colonies here. Hence the legend of Atlantis.

'When the plates on Earth moved, they lost Atlantis which is now in the Antarctic. At that stage of evolution, it was time to leave. But they have kept a close watch ever since.'

Linda asked a few questions followed by a short discussion, and then Dan called for a short break to give Linda a chance to sort out her notes. Ten minutes later, Dan continued with his explanations.

'Now for the last part. On Earth, up to the time of the Industrial Revolution, about two hundred and fifty years ago, everything was fine, except it was the start of pollution. But the Prime Directive, like in the *Star Trek* programme, could not intervene, without revealing themselves. I say these references, Linda, because you did say that you have watched those programmes, so by mentioning them I hope to make it more understandable. If not, please say so.

'The alternative is to give a little kick where technology is slow. A few inventors were given what we called "Starter" information for them to experiment with. Once you have the ball rolling, other people start to improve from the prototypes. No direct contact, it is usually done through a third party. Some inventors are well known, a few were helped along the way. I won't say any more, it would spoil the illusion of history.

55

'Today, there are about five thousand or more Atlanteans living on Earth, leading normal lives in various walks of life. Some are in high or key positions. Their main theme is to observe and report. They have some fifty thousand operatives like Delia and myself. I'm pretty well high up in rank, and I report direct to The Master. Those in the same position as me have their own transport – shuttles, we commonly call them. You will find later that the crew on the mothership use Earth names and references in their dedication. Earth is special to them. Now they are very concerned on how the Earth's environment is deteriorating. Believe it or not, all First World governments have known about the Atlanteans for the past fifty years. They have been warned about the environment situation, but are slow to take steps to improve the planet's health. Earth would happily support four billion people, but, lacking the right technology for six billion people, this will very soon deteriorate.

'We are stepping in because progress is slow. In fact, you know more than most governments. Some are very independent, and will not take any advice from us, saying it is scaremongering and will cause panic if we step in. Others are doing something, but as I said, it's very slow. The point is they don't realise how serious it is becoming. When I say the environment, this covers a wide range – wild animals, trees, the climate change, CO_2, pollution, the sea and the life within it. All this directly or indirectly is causing the Greenhouse Effect. We have to start now if we are going to bring Earth back to health. This will take time, and the deadline is on the horizon. Nature is very strong and now the planet over the last few years is beginning to react.'

Harry then asked, 'What is the answer then, Dad. How are these people you are with going to convince the world's governments to take action?'

'The straight answer is that we, I mean they, will have to step in forcefully if they don't comply. Then the population will know about us, which we do not wish to do yet, because they are not quite ready yet. If the governments do accept our help from our resources, then everything will be OK. Other worlds, which are higher up the evolution ladder, who know about us, have accepted us. Of course, there have been reactions. But they are experienced enough to know how to handle the situation. Earth is due to be enlightened. But not until after the Earth's health has started to improve. Earth is one of five planets that have come to fruition in the last two hundred years, but her environment has brought our plans forward earlier. Fifty years ago we could not do this at all. Completely out of the question. Today we can. Earth's technology has advanced in leaps and bounds, and people's attitude has changed dramatically since the Victorians and especially since the war. There will be unrest, but nothing like it would have been fifty years ago.'

Then Linda asked, 'How are you going to persuade all the governments to co-operate with your intentions?'

'As I said earlier, forcefully to start with, by abduction or kidnapping, whatever word you like to use, Linda. This operation is to bring all the world leaders plus one or more assistant, peacefully, up to the mothership for a massive world conference. That alone will give us their undivided attention. You will learn more about this at a later date. Now I think we will call it a day. The time is now noon. Linda, you are free to ask me questions any time, there's no rush. Later I have plans for you both to meet The Master.'

They had an early lunch. Later, Dan was going to see The Master, to make arrangements for Harry and Linda to meet him, in fact to confirm his report approval on Linda. He had a strong feeling Linda would be OK when they checked her out. Now he was happy with the confirmation. He made the mistake of pushing her when he should have taken it more slowly. Dan had wondered if Linda and Harry would hit it off together; now he could see they had clicked. Both of them needed that break. Dan told them he would be back sometime tomorrow.

To Harry and Linda the rest of the day was their own and the weather was warming up nicely, so Harry suggested going to town by the sea, perhaps to window-shop, anything that came their way, then a meal in the evening.

Linda was happy with his suggestion. She wanted to get away from the house for a while, and the fresh air would clear their heads. Otherwise she would have sat in her bedroom, working on her notes. Linda liked the attention Harry was giving her; he was so different from the other men. Harry, Dan, the commission contract, them up there, she wondered what her stars would have said this week if she had read them.

Forty-five minutes later they had parked in the town, and then took a stroll along the seafront. They walked and talked, learning more about each other. They sat on the beach, looking out to sea and quietly contemplating. They were thinking about Dan's talk, then Linda realised that Dan had not given a date when all this was going to happen. Tomorrow, next year? She mentioned this to Harry.

He replied with, 'Perhaps he doesn't know himself yet.'

Linda then asked Harry his views on the matter in hand.

'I agree with Dad,' he said. 'I know more about the environment, and its workings than most people. Nature is very strong. If something is wrong in one place, it will react in other places, especially if it has been going on for a while. Remember that the Earth is a "living planet". Mother Earth is talking to us. I personally like to see something done. A positive start to put matters right. It will take years to achieve. How? I don't know; maybe they will tell us later.'

How and when? Linda thought; the why, we know. I'll try to put the question to Dan on his return.

*   *   *

They returned to the house about six. As they walked to the kitchen door they noticed the birds singing. They were quite audible now whereas before you took them for granted. Nature and technology, do they mix? One little example and we were blind to it, yet Dan took it into account.

Delia was in the kitchen making cakes, Harry, in Linda's presence, asked her how she made contact with the mother-ship?

'I don't,' answered Delia. 'There's no radio or anything like that, if that's what you mean. This is the first time for many years. But I do know this – I wasn't forgotten. If they needed me, they would have made contact. My job at the time was with your Dad. After he had gone, I suppose I became a "sleeping agent"? There are some things you just cannot explain ... How can I put it ... say, if I were in danger, they would know, that's all I can tell you ... like thought transmission?'

'Mmm,' pondered Harry. 'Thanks, Delia.'

At their favourite pub table, their conversation became more open and more intimate. Linda found she was looking into Harry's blue eyes more deeply, trying to read his thoughts. Although no declaration of love had been made between them, Linda was in love. No bones about it! But what would the future hold for them both, after her commission was com-pletely another question. Harry might decide to go with his Dad. If he wanted her along as well, OK. But what would hap-pen if she didn't like it? Angela, his mother, decided against it.

Linda brought herself out of her deep thoughts: Harry is looking at me. I wait and see what happens, anything could happen, and I'm not going to worry over that now. All I can say is, I've found a man who I love and he has made me feel

59

loved, and there is no better way to gain self-belief and self-confidence. Maybe I was incomplete.

Harry could see that Linda was in deep thought. After a few minutes, she perked up, and the rest of the evening he had her undivided attention.

As they made their way to his car, she got cramp in her thigh again.

Harry helped her to the car and sat her in the front seat with her feet still on the ground. He then proceeded to massage her thigh. 'Hey,' she said in surprise, 'We are not home yet, you know!' Just as she said those words, another couple strolled by to the next car. Although it was an innocent move by Harry, Linda was embarrassed by the outward appearance of a compromising situation. He was laughing, and Linda saw the funny side and started to giggle as she pulled her skirt straight.

He parked in the barn alongside Linda's car and leaned over to her and gave her a long passionate kiss. She responded eagerly. 'Reminds me of my courting days,' she said, passionately and out of breath. 'We'd better go in,' she said, after a few minutes, 'Delia will think there is something wrong.'

'She is not that innocent, you know, she is a hot-blooded woman,' informed Harry.

'Has Delia got a boyfriend?' asked Linda curiously.

'She has. He comes up to visit her two, maybe three times a week. If she is free at the weekends, he takes her out. Of course, when I'm home, it's not so often. She has known him for some years now.' He started to kiss her again. 'Let's go to bed,' whispered Linda.

Inside the house, all was dark and quiet, except for the usual light in the kitchen. 'There's no light from Delia's flat. She is having an early night, by the looks of it,' stated Harry.

They went upstairs quietly. After a few minutes, they were

in bed. Linda was rubbing her thigh. 'Have you got cramp again?' enquired Harry.

'No,' she said, 'The muscle at the back of the leg is stiff, it keeps niggling me.'

'Turn over,' said Harry, 'I will give you a proper massage this time.'

Linda's eyes lit up and she did as she was told, without saying a word.

Harry started to massage the back of her thigh gently, pressing his thumbs deep into the flesh, feeling for the troublesome muscle. Then he warned her, that he was now going to press harder, and to try to bear the treatment, if possible for a little while. Linda clenched her teeth and grasped the pillow with her hands. Harry felt the muscle relax slowly. 'All over,' he said. Linda was relieved: that was painful, she thought, but she felt much better, the stiffness had gone, for the time being anyway.

Then Harry proceeded to stroke and slightly tickle her shoulders, back and down her spine. Mmm, that's nice, she said to herself, and became relaxed for the welcome relief. Then she felt quite aroused as he continued. Her breathing came quicker and faster. Harry's hands then went to her bottom, lingered there for a while, teasing her with his fingertips, stroking and caressing the cheeks. Now Linda was moaning for more, as she squirmed to his touch and at the same time, begging him to stop. Teasingly, he did stop.

'No, don't stop,' she gasped as she tried to look at the man she loved over her shoulder. For a second, her eyes were saying, what are you doing to me? But she did not try to stop him, just moaned louder and gave in to his penetrating caresses. She drew her knees up under her body and ended up on all fours, then she went down on to her elbows. Then his fingers did the talking as they slowly crept up the inside of her thighs.

'Oooh ... yoou ... sod!' cried Linda, gasping as she buried

61

her face into the pillow to stifle her cries. She then surrendered, stating her submission to him.

Then Harry took her, as the one word between her breathless gasps was demanding, NOW! . . . Nooow.

That night, Linda gave in to a man, her man, in a very different way and he possessed her. Never before had she been that intimate and reached such heights of ecstasy.

Afterwards, he held Linda in his arms, the only woman ever in his life to light up his soul.

Then she quietly said, looking up to him, 'I love you,' before she fell into an exhausted and contented sleep.

4

Linda awoke to a knock on the bedroom door. She quickly glanced at Harry; he was dead to the world. There was a pause as she thought of being seen in Harry's bed. Then came another knock. With a hesitant voice, she answered, 'Come in.'

The door opened and Delia came in with two cups of tea on a tray with the post and paper under her arm. Not batting an eyelid, she said, 'Sorry to intrude, but it is eight o'clock, so I thought I'd bring you both a cup of tea in bed.'

Linda just lay there; she saw her nightie on the chair by the bed. With only her eyes peering over the sheets, she watched Delia place the tray on the bedside cabinet. As Delia left the room, Linda looked at her watch: it is eight, and we've overslept. Now she could get out of bed. Then Harry sat up, laughing to himself as he reached out for his cup. Then Linda clicked. 'You weren't asleep,' she said. 'You were pretending, you sod,' then punched him playfully on his arm. With her expressive smiling face, she stated, 'You love teasing me!'

'Only because I love you, Linda.'

'Oh,' she said, at his enlightening reply. She put her arms around his neck and kissed him. 'That's nice, Harry, thank you. You don't know how much that means to me.'

Later, they sat in the garden, enjoying the warmth of the sun.

It is out early today, not a cloud in sight. 'No sign of Dad, I wonder what time he'll be back,' pondered Harry as he read the paper. 'We ought to have some kind of communication in case we need to contact him.'

He put the paper down, then looked at Linda. He was thinking erotically; funny how women can tease, without having to say a word. I bet God had a good knowing laugh to himself when he brought Eve along as a mate for Adam. He brought himself back to reality and said, 'While I have got the chance, Linda, I think I will finalise my report for work this evening. In the meantime there are a few odd jobs to do. Is that all right with you?'

'OK. It will give me a chance to sort my notes out and compose my story.'

After lunch, there was still no appearance of Dan's return. They decided to go into the village. Here Harry collected the items he needed to complete his jobs.

On returning home, there was still no sign of Dan, so Harry asked Delia if they could have dinner earlier than usual. This would give them more time for their planned working evening.

By midnight Harry had completed his final report. Although the report was not required until August, he would send it off tomorrow – that would surprise them, he was usually late. Now he can forget about it. There were more important personal matters to attend to. He went to his bedroom and saw Linda's light was still on in her room at the end of the landing. He wondered how she was progressing. He didn't want to disturb her if she was in full flow. But curiosity got the better of him and he slowly opened the door and peeked in. She was sitting on the bed with papers covering the bed and some were on the floor. She appeared very busy and he decided not to disturb her.

She looked up from her papers on seeing him, smiled and said, 'Nearly there, be finished in a few minutes.' She started to gather up her paperwork so she could file it in order.

'If I can do this as I go along, it will make life easier for me later, then all I have to do is type them up when I return home.' She then paused to comment, 'Do you realise this is the story of the century, a world exclusive.' Another pause, realising, 'Oh dear, I suppose I probably will have to go into hiding with a story like this – the girl who went into space and who met another race!'

'Do you want me to make you a drink as you clear up?'

'Oh yes please, Delia brought me one up earlier, I always find paperwork is thirsty work.'

You must be in Delia's good books, I didn't get one, thought Harry, there again, Delia knows I don't like to be disturbed when I'm very busy in the evenings. The thought of Linda going into hiding did not occur to him: I'm sure it won't be that drastic, anyway she'll be looked after.

A little while later, as they prepared for bed, Linda was pleased she was up to date with her story. At that moment in time, she was in her element. With Dan being away it gave her the opportunity to catch up, and to organise herself an inventory on certain important questions for clarification.

Linda cuddled up to Harry.

'Everything all right?' asked Harry.

'Yes,' replied Linda with a mischievous look in her eyes, a slight pause, then quietly, 'except that muscle is still niggling me...'

Tuesday

Early next morning, Linda went to the bathroom and returned wearing her nightie. Slipping in alongside Harry

65

she dozed until he stirred, then cuddled up to him, mainly to wake him up. Linda wasn't getting up and out of bed this time until Harry had his feet on the floor.

Linda was half-expecting Delia to enter the room with a tray. Harry stirred and turned to look at Linda and gave her an early morning kiss. He noticed the nightie and her eyes watching the door.

'Not today, Linda,' he whispered, reading her face. 'You are free to get dressed.' He yawned and made a statement, which made Linda's ears prick up. 'Anyway, you're not the Lady of the House – yet!'

Is that a subtle hint? thought Linda, or is he joking again. She watched him, wondering, as he, half-asleep, staggered for the shower. 'You ought to lay off your nightly midnight prenuptial nutrients, you look awful,' her own words surprised Linda: they just came out, clear and precise.

'That's love for you, Linda,' said a raised voice from the shower. 'Just making up for lost time.'

'Well, he's awake anyway, to catch those words.' That's the second time he said love ... I wonder if that hint is genuine? She dashed to the bathroom. 'HEY! What do you mean, making up for lost time ...'

It was a dull chilly morning; Linda put on a cardigan over her T-shirt. After breakfast, they sat in the sitting room, Harry reading his post while Linda read through the paper. Then she remembered she should have rung her friend to say she had no idea when she would be back for their weekly night out. Linda went out to the kitchen to make the call.

A little later, a call on her mobile came through. The call came from the magazine concerning her latest article. They liked the story. They would like to bring the date forward, to print in the August edition. Linda told them to hold, as Mr Kent was on the other line, and quickly conferred with Harry. He said it was OK by him. He had read the story. Linda told them, in her business voice, Mr Kent is happy with the August publication. Harry was pulling faces at her. She had to terminate the call quickly.

Linda sat on his lap, took his face into her hands and said to him, 'One of these days I'm going to get my own back on you!' He put his hand to the nape of her neck and held her there as he kissed her on those pouting lips as she finished saying the word you. 'And I, my sweet, one of these days, I'm going to smack that lovely bottom of yours!'

'You wouldn't DARE!' said she, shocked.

'Then don't dare me, because I like a challenge,' smiling at her. Linda was temporarily lost for words, then said, 'If any other man had said those words, he wouldn't have got away with it.'

'I know. Masterful, aren't I?' He then changed the subject. 'I wonder what is keeping Dad?'

The door opened and Delia came in with a plate of cakes and placed them on the table.

'Well, talking of the Devil,' said Delia, 'I think he has just turned up,'

'How do you know that?' asked Linda.

'As he is expected back, I kept my mobile on the table in the kitchen, so when the signal goes dead, it can only mean one thing.'

'What a clever idea, Delia. I should have thought of that!' said Harry.

'At best,' stated Delia, 'it should give you about two minutes' warning.' They went out into the garden and waited. About a minute later, Dan appeared from the side of the house. He looked surprised by the welcoming committee. Harry explained. Dan gave a laugh, 'Not for much longer, they are working on that inconvenience. We can't have the mobiles dead, especially Linda's. She is the only one who should be in contact with the outside world with her mobile, her work and relatives.'

'So why are you late? You were due back yesterday.'

'Sorry, unexpected extra work,' replied Dan. 'The Master has arranged for you two to visit the mothership, he wants to meet you both and explain the situation, especially to Linda.'

'When do we go?' enquired Harry.

'Early this afternoon, you will be back tomorrow. So an overnight bag is all you need.'

'Is it dangerous, this teleporting thing?' asked Linda, looking a bit worried.

'It can be, but only over a long distance. There is nothing to worry about. I will explain it to you both in simple terms. But now, shall we go indoors, I miss Delia's tea and cakes.'

You are two of a kind, thought Linda, then the butterflies inside her started to raise their wings again Stepping into the unknown, it's not everyday you meet an alien race!

About an hour before leaving they all gathered in the sitting room, to listen to some information about matter teletransportation, as Dan would not have time later to explain the basic principles.

'First of all, all questions will be answered in the simplest form – the basics. There's no need to know more unless you want to be a student on the subject. Like your mobile phone, you understand the basics, and that is as far as it has to go with most people. Behind every answer, there lies complicated technology with many thousands of years of research behind it . . . leave it at that.

'Teleporting started in its infancy by listening to sound as it travels. Light travels at a much faster speed. Sound is made to go further and faster with the telephone to a designated destination by wire. Then radio waves were transmitted without the wire, but unless channelled they went everywhere, even with a receiver station, and everybody could eavesdrop, unless coded. Later, radio waves were beamed to a certain point, using different and higher frequencies. So you now can send sound and images, like your TV for example. But you cannot transmit matter. That is the ultimate ball game. Signals go everywhere and, so would matter if not controlled; it has to be beamed from the sending station to the receiving station. That is the complicated part, which frequencies, how much energy, and to start with the formula to break down the atoms of the subject to be transmitted and put together in its original form at the receiving end without damage. This took aeons to perfect. Before the Atlanteans arrived on Earth, this particular technology reached its infinite perfection. Now you just walk through a portal; the atoms in your body are not broken up, as I mentioned earlier. Also, I would like to add that the Atlanteans and the Nacanians are the only people to have this technology.'

Linda wanted a bit more definition about the dangers involved.

'You really are nervous about this, aren't you Linda?' said Dan, understanding her dilemma. 'Let me reassure you there is absolutely no danger involved. Short-distance travel is no problem. The long distance is like radio waves dissipating into space, even when beamed. Like a torch beam fading into the darkness unless it hits something solid. This applies only to light year travel, perhaps I wasn't clear enough in my meaning of danger. To overcome this technicality over distance, they put booster buoys, one for every light year of travel. It was as simple as that. For example, from here to Alpha Centauri – it's a star group, Linda, before you ask,' anticipating her questioning looks. 'The distance to there is between four and five light years if you travel at light speed. Lower the speed, the longer it takes. They can cover that distance in seconds! With the help of four transmitters – booster buoys in line, plus of course, a receiving station. Originally, in any first exploration, you have to get there in the first place to set up a receiving station, and that takes a long time to achieve. Like our early sea explorers, they were away for years. Now in travelling, it is just hours in most cases. That is happening now, these people are exploring the unknown on the far side of the galaxy.'

Linda was still puzzled how matter is transmitted.

'Don't concern yourself over the technicalities on this point, Linda, it's far to complicated. Just think of a person throwing a ball to another person, one is a transmitter, the other is the receiver. Matter is being transported from A to B and so on. The speed and the technology involved, I'm afraid to say, are all beyond us mere mortals. My ship above can transfer a person down by using the ground as an earth. The power in my ship I cannot explain. All I need to know is that it is powered by some device in the form of anti-gravity, with matter and anti-matter energy. In simple terms, you just point and go.'

Dan gave a long pause to let things sink in, then said, 'We will be leaving in an hour, to give you time to prepare.'

Upstairs, Linda and Harry packed a few things together in two overnight bags. Harry included a camera, while Linda made sure she had tapes and batteries. Then, which clothes to wear and what to pack. Dan had said earlier to make sure they had comfortable walking shoes.

Linda paraded for Harry for approval. 'My god, you look gorgeous, I feel sorry for the males up there. Haven't you got a looser top than that?' looking at her bosom. 'No,' said Linda, and teasingly walked slowly towards him, kissed him on the cheek, and said quietly, but distinctly, as she passed by him with her bag, 'GIRL POWER!'

They returned to the sitting room as arranged. Linda asked if Delia was coming with them. Dan said, 'No, she is up to date with the details, I briefed her the other night, her job is to be here. Anyway, she doesn't like fairground rides.'

'Oh, thanks,' said Linda.

' Only joking,' said Dan, 'Delia is just one of those people who suffers badly from air and sea as well as space sickness.'

They are ready to go. Linda grabbed Harry's hand and held it tight. He squeezed her hand reassuringly. Dan spoke into his wrist device.

'Right, I go first, in a few seconds after I've gone, you will follow . . . relax, there's nothing to it.'

He spoke again, giving an order this time, into the wrist device. Then he was gone. Linda closed her eyes tight, as if she had reached the brow of the Big Dipper.

Nothing happened, something was wrong! Then a voice spoke to her; it sounded distant.

'You can open your eyes now,' said Dan. She opened her eyes and saw a different environment surrounding her. Harry had to ungrasp her hand from his. 'You have to get those nails trimmed, if we're going to have this every time. Look, you have drawn blood.' He smiled at her and put his other hand around her shoulder. 'Well how was it? Did the earth move for you? he continued, joking.

'Is that it! Is that all there is to it?' said Linda, her voice nervously high, 'Nothing to it!' trying to look as if she enjoyed it and composing herself at the same time.

Harry and Linda looked around them, taking in their new surroundings.

They found they were in an enclosed sphere-shaped room, with smooth light reflecting walls. A couch-type seat at one end and a door. At the other end they saw Dan, by a control console with one seat, which they presumed to be the pilot's seat.

Between them and Dan were four seats, in a tandem of two, the type you find on a passenger airliner. Dan invited them to sit in the front two seats. They sat down and Dan warned them they might have a reaction to their experience, but it would pass quickly. If they did it would be the only time they would have it. Delia was the exception; she got it all the time. For a second, Linda felt dizzy and nauseous. Harry never felt anything, except the feeling of heavy feet.

Dan swivelled on his seat to face the console. He spoke, but not to them, 'Observation screen please, 180 degrees.' There within their eye vision, the wall in front of them turned into a view of the surrounding countryside. Dan turned his ship around to face the south towards the sea. Harry and Linda were enthralled by the silence they did not expect, just a slight low humming. Dan told them that they were automatically held in their seats if anything happened. They could get up to walk about if they wished.

They were still stationary over the house. Dan spoke to the console again. 'You may speak, Judi, we are returning to the mothership. Authorisation code, Zero. 6/4, voice check.'

'Authorisation confirmed,' said a female voice coming from the console.

Linda sat there amused, smiling to herself. Harry was also grinning.

'Dad, I can't believe what I'm hearing. A computer that speaks to you, and a woman's voice as well.'

'I take it you approve, then. Judi is in control of the ship; I just give her instructions. I can go manual if I wish, but she will take over if there's any danger.'

'Judi, did you say?' said Harry, 'She has a name as well?'

'Hello, Harry and Linda, I hope you enjoy your trip. Yes, my name is Judi. Do you not approve?'

'I approve. Just surprised, that's all.'

'I know that voice,' said Linda, still amused. 'I've got it now, I know who that is. Now, I don't believe it.'

Harry interrupted, 'Well, who is it? I don't recognise the voice.'

'It sounds like Judi Dench, you old rascal, Dan,' said Linda. 'You have to explain this to us.'

'You are right, Linda, computers are controlled by voice instructions. The crews are given a choice of voices. Overall, the men choose a female, and the women, a male voice. They get to know each other for a more relaxed atmosphere.'

'Did you say women?' said Linda 'You have got women up there?'

'Yes, of course we have, didn't I say? I think you are going to be surprised, Linda. Now, I think we had better make a move, just relax and enjoy.'

Dan instructed Judi to go straight for the sea, then up to the mothership. 'We usually go straight up, but as it's your first time, we will give you a gentler ride.'

The ship started to move towards the sea, with no sensation of moving at all, but the land below was flashing past fast. In a few seconds they were out over the sea, suddenly the horizon dropped below them, the view they had, turned to blue sky and they were now climbing vertically. The sky then turned black. Then the stars came shining through. What NASA would give for this ship! thought Harry.

Dan then instructed Judi for a 360-degree view from their cabin. Harry had already sat himself down on the seat, after experiencing the fast climb into space. He thought he would have been thrown severely to the rear of the ship, but Dan told him to just walk normally to his seat, which he did, but still held the back of the seat instinctively. He couldn't believe he was still upright. He did not feel any different, as if he was walking around his front room. Linda had her eyes shut, not tight this time, but if the arms of her seat had veins, it would have been bleeding to death. Linda opened her eyes and blinked in relief.

They could not take in how short the journey took in time to reach space. Harry, on hearing the instruction for Judi, swivelled on his seat to face to the rear. Linda followed suit. They both wanted to see this unmissable event.

There before them was Earth. The awesome sight that greeted them 'live' was limited to a privileged few, they, who came from this beautiful world! They stood up, held hands and took in this wonder. Earth was in full sunlight. The colours were bright and clear. Harry quickly took out his camera for the memento. Then Harry asked Linda to stand in front of him, with the Earth, high to one side of her. Dan offered to take some photos of them together, with the Earth above their heads.

Judi reminded Dan, that they were approaching the mothership. They all returned quickly to their seats. Harry spoke first, 'I can't see anything! Where is it?' He wanted to take more pictures of this unbelievable sight. Linda wondered if they would be permitted to print them in the book. 'You won't see her just yet,' informed Dan. 'Her shields protect her and also make the ship invisible.'

All Harry and Linda could see was blackness, yet she must be right in front of them.

'Automatic docking procedure in process,' announced Judi.

Dan switched on the viewer and called them   up to observe the sight on the screen. 'Through the viewer only,' he said, 'before we pass through the perimeter of the shields, you will see my home for the last thirty years.' Thirty seconds later, they passed through the shields, then through the observation screens a clearer portrayal of the mothership came into view.

This was another wonder to look at. Harry managed to get in a couple of shots.

'Oh my God,' stated Linda, 'I didn't expect this. She is kind of, oh, I know, what's the word for it . . .'

'A dodecahedron is the word you're looking for,' cut in Dan. 'That's it, a twelve-sided polyhedron.'

'Oh look! She's opalescent, blue . . . and a yellow, what's causing that, Dan?' asked Linda.

'A natural phenomenon,' informed Dan. 'The light creates the colours from the rays from the sun, coming through the shields. The twelve planes are there for technological purposes.'

'She looks huge – how big is she?' asked Harry in awe, in

between the odd reports from the running docking procedures from Judi.

She is three miles in circumference and about one in diameter,' answered Dan. 'Those dashes of black lines around the centre are the docking areas.'

As they came nearer, the brief reports became more frequent. Dan was just watching the procedures.

'Looks like a busy place,' said Harry, watching other vessels coming and going.

'You'd be surprised how busy,' answered Dan. 'If it's of any interest to you, we all have our own docking bays. We are approaching ours now.'

They went slowly through one of the holes in a row of six, one of many rows that continued around the centre of the mothership. The docking bay appeared small at first, but as they passed through, it seemed to open up and swallowed them. Dan then told Harry that there was a half a mile of ship above them, as well as below.

They left their ship through the door at the rear of the cabin. Here they passed a small room to another door at the rear and stepped down onto the docking platform.

Linda asked what was in the space between the two doors. Dan whispered in her ear.

'Oh,' she said. 'Thank you, now I know where to go.'

Harry and Linda viewed the spacious docking area as they made their way to the reception and security area, before being allowed into the interior of the mothership.

They also saw for the first time the design of their spacecraft they just arrived in.

They stood and took in the shape. They wondered how one would describe a craft like this to anybody who wanted to know.

The best they could come up with is a sort of a longitudinal sphere, about thirty feet in length overall, a shiny smooth moulded surface with no visible doors or windows.

Dan informed them that the official names for these little ships were pods – the children of the mothership, but they preferred shuttles. Their next stop on the agenda was to meet The Master.

They followed Dan through the precautionary airlock door, which automatically slid open on approaching. They only operated as airlocks, when the air pressure in the docking area dropped. On passing through they found themselves in a very wide round seamless corridor, running parallel with the docking ring around the ship. In the corridor, on the far side, was a monorail type of transport, capsules that carry about six people at a time. Fitted flush to the far wall and separated from the walkway by a one-step-up narrow platform, the capsules could stop anywhere, but usually at lead-off corridors, lifts or stairways on the right. The capsules travelled in one direction only, with about a one minute gap between each capsule. To go in the opposite direction, there was an identical corridor above this one. It had to be this way, because these corridors were the busiest part of the ship, with people going about on their various duties, like cargo goods being transferred, passengers and maintenance, etc. They came to a junction, and transferred to another capsule. This one went across the one-mile width of the ship, all connected to a maze of normal corridors, lifts and stairways. It was all very confusing to any newcomers. But there was a simple solution to this, if not accompanied with someone. All the crew were in uniform. Anybody in civilian clothes came under the authority of The Master.

They arrived at the heart of the ship; Dan led the way to a lift, here Dan was stopped by Security. Although they knew him, they had to check Harry and Linda. All was OK, as they had received passes on arrival at reception. The lift was smooth and fast. Dan told them that they operated by Antigravity, no cables. Linda was glad she was informed after they stepped out!

They arrived at The Master's operation complex of administration. So far, Linda and Harry had been impressed by the environmental status. They expected claustrophobic conditions. Instead everywhere was bright and airy, very spacious, and the décor gave any bareness you would expect in a space station of this size, a soothing and relaxed atmosphere. The illumination and colours appearing to come from within the walls were pleasing and tranquil. The Master's operational suite was like any other office. With Dan behind them, two ladies greeted Linda and Harry. They introduced themselves as Eva and Lesley, The Master's PA's in everything. They were highly respected and held no rank, but as The Master's Lieutenants, everybody obeyed their instructions.

Linda has noticed on the way here, that there were plenty of women around, many in uniform.

Eva showed them through to The Master's office. They saw a man sitting at what appeared to be his desk, a white moulded top that curved in a half-circle around him. He seemed to have plenty of paperwork cluttering his desktop. He arose from his work immediately and came around to greet them. Linda saw that he was a tall, well-built, white-haired man. The Master appeared to be about the same age as Dan. But as Eva handed him his white, hooded cloak denoting his standing of authority within the ship's community, Linda guessed that he was much older.

Linda had been informed earlier that this race's life-span was considerably longer and that they were more active than the people of Earth in their mature years. His gravelly voice reminded her of the actor Joss Ackland. Later, after the formal introductions, he dispensed with the cloak while in his domain of the operations suite.

'Sorry, I could not meet you on your arrival, I was held up, so I thought it best to meet you here: Linda and Harry, I'm very pleased to meet you both at last. Dan has kept me up to date over the last few days. I have invited you up here so that you will understand the big picture, and for me to explain everything to you. I will give you a few details now, and later, over dinner this evening, the finer details.'

He invited them to sit on one of three leather sofas, which were out of sight around the corner of his large 'L'-shaped office. Here they saw a magnificent view from a large outward protruding 'bubble' window. The Earth was in full view. Linda and Harry stood in the bay of the bubble, absorbing and partly hypnotised by the inspiring view. They could see the North Pole but not the South Pole. Linda enquired how far they were from the Earth? Fifty thousand miles, came the reply from the Master, and never directly between the Earth and the sun, always a few degrees off. They were in stationary position above the Earth, with the Earth rotating before them. The ship's clocks are on GMT. They settled down to talk, the seats in a semi-circle facing the view.

Linda and Harry were silent, except for small talk and the odd question. Both of them were still taking in the wonder of the ship; they were certainly not expecting the scenes they were seeing. Dan never gave a hint of what they would encounter; perhaps he wanted to surprise them, or more realistically, he in no way could explain something out of this world. One of many reasons why they were invited up here was, as The Master had stated, to get the full picture!

In the hour and a half they were with The Master, he gave them, in half of that time, the low-down on various matters. Lesley, in the meantime, gave Linda a contract, a bond concerning her commission, to be signed later, and a replacement for her tape recorder – she was informed that no batteries were required or any need for her to plug in, ever – plus a number of small versions of recording discs with two hours' recording time.

At the introductory meeting, Linda and Harry learned that the mothership had a crew of 4,000 and that half the crew were women!

'Is that because of sexual equality?' queried Linda.

'That question has never entered the equation,' answered The Master. 'It is simply all down to qualifications and natural capability, then we equal them out for postings, like here, for instance.'

Linda persevered further with a few simple questions, just to clarify some minor points, while she had the chance. Then Harry put in a quick one.

'I would have thought the crew complement for the size of this ship would have been higher?'

The Master hesitated for a moment.

'Let me say, we have more than enough crew on board. This ship may look big to you, but each member of crew does have their own quarters on the upper and lower decks, plus a further five hundred rooms are available for diplomatic personnel. People like yourselves and for Earth helpers, like your father, of whom there are many, who are coming and going all the time. Also all the sophisticated systems we have do take up a large amount of space. There are nearly a hundred and fifty shuttles plus six larger freighter berths. Then there are six dining areas, an evening restaurant, and gyms. A very large Kew-styled garden – I recommend both of you, to go and see that. The power drive sector ... need I go on, Harry?' said The Master, his eyebrows lifting instead of smiling.

'Er ... no, thank you, I see your point,' murmured Harry. He hadn't expected such a detailed answer.

Towards the end of the meeting, The Master told them about the peace talks, the environment, jungle clearances, o-zone and pollution problems, and the world leaders meeting up here – no date for this yet. Then he went on to another big problem they had. Dan had mentioned this briefly, earlier.

'As you know, I am in charge of the Earth Project. We have been here in strength for the past one hundred and fifty years, the beginnings of our concern for Earth's future, but the Nacanians have been here in force as well. Their world is situated in the constellation of Taurus, the Seven Sisters group of stars, known as the Pleiades. There is another ship like this – her sister ship – they are in that area now, four hundred light years away, dealing with that, hence the UFO sightings you have had over the last fifty years. When we catch them at their game, they go, because they know we will obliterate them if they fire upon us. This cold war is getting out of control, so we have plans for them as well, but in a different way. I'm afraid to say we may have to eradicate this race. We are in negotiations with them, but there is not much hope of anything good coming out the meetings. This will be the first failure in our history.'

Linda asked The Master, 'What is the main agenda with them in your negotiations?'

'We have offered them a "New World" in another star system, which we were preparing to populate in our expansion of the galaxy. Even with our help to settle in every way, they have turned this offer down because they want Earth! They have visited other worlds in their limited explorations, but none have come up to Earth standards.

'What it all boils down to is, we are saving one world, but in the process we may have to destroy another.

'I tell you now; they are the cesspit of this galaxy! We have tried to "cleanse" them, but we cannot until they have moved. Besides air and gravity on Earth, their world has a third element, a genetic make-up of evil, which we did not know about until it was too late. This third element increases as the population grows, feeding on them. I think Dan told you they were one of the first planets we populated, and we failed to keep a proper watch on them. It was our mistake in the first place! So we are putting every effort into the negotiations. If they had accepted, we would have then decontaminated the old planet so that there is nothing left of its influences then, in time, renewed life there. I fear failure, because they have mutated.

'Many of our people have died in negotiations with them over the years, and our peaceful stance is coming to an end, for we have to protect the other worlds from their evil before it is too late. That is why you are here, Linda, to observe and write on these two problems for the record as an independent writer, starting only a few days ago on a story you knew nothing about or existed ... I end there for now. If you all care to have dinner with me tonight, I will explain further.'

A few minutes later, Eva introduced them to Sarah, who was waiting in the outer office. Sarah, they were told, would show them to their room and take care of them. 'You are free to wander to the observation gallery. Later if you wish, Sarah will give you a guided tour of the ship, but only with her as a chaperone. You may use your camera, Harry, but not in any restricted areas.'

Sarah showed them around their room and the bathroom, what buttons to press and not to press. 'If you are not sure, just say clearly, "Computer, lights on or off". The same with the heating or ventilation, then the computer will ask, to what degree? If you haven't already said so, you'll soon get the hang of it.'

Sarah seemed to be about 18 to 20, a cheerful, bubbly young woman with pretty looks with her blonde wavy hair nearly to her shoulders, about the same height as Linda. All staff under The Master wore civilian clothes, including Eva and Lesley. Linda also had the impression they were following Earth's fashions. Sarah answered their queries amiably. She said she would be back in an hour, after they had settled in, for their tour of the ship.

Linda turned to Harry and said, with a glint in her eye, 'I wonder why they gave us one room to share?'

'It appears they know everything about us, even about the camera in my bag. I will now take as many photos as possible.'

Linda checked her new recorder; she listened for a minute or two, and was very impressed with the quality of the sound – far better than her own, expensive model. She put her old one back in her bag. Then together, they nosed around their room. Linda tried the bed, 'Mmm, this is nice.' Harry sat on the other side. Before she knew it, Linda was lying down with Harry bestowing her with kisses, cuddles and pillow talk.

An hour later, Sarah returned for their guided tour. She gave them some information sheets, with some Do's and Don'ts. 'That will not apply to you,' she informed them with a cheeky grin, 'as you will be accompanied by me, yours truly.'

Before leaving, Sarah explained to them that when they retired to bed, if they wished, they could have induced into their minds a brief history and culture of their civilisation. When they awoke, they would have more understanding and knowledge of Sarah's race. 'You don't have to accept the inducement if you don't wish to, but I would personally advise you both to have the experience.'

Harry then enquired of Sarah, 'What is this ... inducement method ... into the mind, we have heard this word mentioned before by Dad?'

Sarah's reply enlightened them. 'It is an educational method used on our children for schooling. Instead of homework or study every night, students preferred to use this method, about twice a week on average. Then next day they have a test on the selected subject to see how they are progressing. This helps the understanding of their studies, as our advance technology is at its infinite in this galaxy, and students need all the help available in their studies. For the slow learners, used regularly, this method brings them up to grade.'

Linda and Harry wanted to learn more about this race, without having to ask too many awkward questions. So with their curiosity, as well as having the experience to see how much wiser they would be in the morning, they decided to have the inducement on their overnight stay.

'I'm glad you have agreed to accept the experience,' said Sarah. 'I will show you how, on your room computer tonight. Now, are you ready for your tour?'

'We are,' said Harry with enthusiasm. 'We are looking forward to seeing the ship very much.'

Sarah replied with a sigh, 'We have only two hours for the tour, so today I'll show you the main interesting places, then next time, you name it and I will take you there. You were with The Master longer than expected. So I'll give my apologies now for the delay.'

So for the next two hours, Linda and Harry followed Sarah through the maze of corridors. This area was the main operations of the ship concerning Earth. Except for the occasional reminder in her notes, Linda held Harry's arm or hand, not for being nervous, but for being enthralled and for her love for Harry and her own enthusiasm for the privilege for being up here. Linda now accepted the situation. She liked Sarah and the consoling thought that there were women on board. This was the future. The environment was totally different from what she had expected. She felt safe. The butterflies were asleep.

On their tour, they got to know each other more. Linda was right about the women's fashions, they did copy Earth, and some were especially ordered and brought up by shuttle, via the helpers, as were fruit and vegetables, meat and other commodities that made life more pleasurable. Also the adopted use of Earth's Christian names of their choice. They covered, surprisingly, nearly all Sarah had planned for them in the allotted time, using stairs, escalators, the anti-gravity lifts and moving sidewalks in busy areas, used mainly for movement of cargo. Some corridors even had a keep left or right policy in force. Sarah took them through the surveillance and sensor departments. The computers and other hi-tech equipment were way beyond their understanding. All the computers on board 'talked' to each other, sharing information, so the left hand did know what the right hand was up to.

This ship had plenty of entertainment, a whole deck, delegated to games of every description, plus a few unheard of. At the front entrance to Kew Gardens, they had a quick view, but no time to explore as the gardens took up the space of six decks with a walk-around-viewing gallery and extended for a quarter of a mile. This went to the top of the list for a must-see next time. This was a similar version of Central Park in New York, where people went to walk and relax. Below this was the Engineering section, the power source. This took up a quarter of a mile in the dead centre of the ship. This was one of three places they were prohibited to enter, but maybe later, said Sarah, under the Captain's discretion. The other two were the control centre – the Bridge – and a place named simply the Airport Lounge. At these locations there was a high security presence.

The main off-duty theme was socialising; otherwise you could become isolated. Leave was plentiful. The crew could stay as long as they liked, one month to a lifetime, which was thirty years' service. Nobody over that age could stay on unless they were of high rank or authority. Sarah also informed Linda and Harry that it was a happy ship. Always had been.

The crew's vocation on this ship was of a high dedication for the welfare of Earth. The motto amongst the crew was 'If you can walk, walk and achieve your goal.' The majority of people on board were from Anthena with a few aliens from other advanced worlds. All wore uniforms according to their professions.

Sarah was a gem to have as a guide and escort, answering all questions clearly, no matter how trivial. Later, she showed them back to their quarters; Linda and Harry were relieved at last to put up their aching feet. Both of them felt they had walked miles.

The answer to the questions 'how and when' was still to come.

After resting, Sarah led them to The Master's quarters for dinner, they met Dan en route. There Sarah left them. This time, they were greeted by The Master himself. Linda pondered further for a moment on his age, but there was no telling, at a guess that he was well advanced in years, as Dan now looked younger with his service up here.

They were looked after and served by Lesley and Eva on behalf of their host.

Harry stated that Atlanteans seemed to be taller, judging from the members of the crew he had seen so far.

The Master replied that Harry had observed correctly. The population on Anthena were on average two inches taller than the people on Earth, due to the fact that Anthena was slightly bigger, but had less gravity. This affected all people in various ways, depending on which world they came from.

Harry continued with another question, 'When I'm on Earth and looking up to the stars, where do I look to find Anthena?' The Master thought for a moment. 'An interesting question. We are in the Scorpius Constellation, next door to Sagittarius which is towards the centre of the Milky Way looking from Earth. We are near the star Antares. Our world is about six hundred light years from here. To answer your question further, we rise in the night sky from the Southern Hemisphere when Orion and the Pleiades set in the north, so Earth is about halfway between these two star systems, let's say in round figures about a thousand light years from one star system to the other. There's no life towards the galaxy centre, as it is too dense and the stars are much younger. We have populated about sixty worlds on the Earth's side of the galaxy. Most of them are in the outer rings of the spiral. We have also populated a second "Anthena" ourselves. Our race has not reached the opposite side of the Milky Way yet, but we are getting there, expanding all the time. The galaxy is so vast, a hundred thousand light years across. You never know, there might be another race there, exploring with the same attention as us.' The Master stopped for a few moments. Then he continued, 'This may surprise you, we experimented with DNA on certain primates at one time, to see if intelligent life would evolve in Africa from the gorilla, chimps and selected monkeys. But nothing came out of the tests. The chimp, incidentally, came from our world.'

Harry was surprised by this statement; it explained certain answers to many certain questions.

'I hope you found the tour enlightening,' said The Master, continuing his explanation of some unanswered questions for Linda's notes. 'I'm informed that you reached the Airport Lounge; sorry you were not allowed to enter there. Even the crew are not permitted unless you have a travel pass. It is not the sort of place to be wandering around in; it can be very dangerous with the very sophisticated complex technology involved. The place means what it says, for people to travel. I shall take you there later when I have arranged a trip for you. To put it simply, in there is a large Portal – a doorway for you to pass through. You can see the reception area on the other side of the Portal, it's usually home on our world six hundred light years away.' Oh no, now what? thought Linda. This frightened her, 600 light years across open space.

The butterflies in her stomach were not stirring this time, they were having a riot! Then she thought of Harry and his hand to hold. She felt better after that comforting consolation of his presence. Linda wondered at times, if Harry wasn't in the picture – would she be coping as well as she was now? It was a pondering dilemma of two possible scenarios. Linda's thoughts were interrupted when The Master began to speak again; she noticed he was looking at her, was he reading her concerns? Anyway, it might be a short trip to another ship or to Earth for some reason, consoling and fooling herself at the same time ...

'Officially, we call them the "Space Dimension Portals" but the crew adopted the name, Travel Gate, a variation taken from the films on Earth, like Gate, Time Gate etc. To travel this way is only possible over very long distances by using booster stations, one for every one light year between A and B. Wormholes don't work very well, especially for life forms – they are very unstable, even with our technology. So in the end we created our own wormholes: far safer and quicker in the long run. Incidentally, from the start, we had these Travel Gates on Earth, like Avebury. But we had to stop using them about two thousand years ago, as the locals became too curious. This also applied to other places like Mexico, South America, Egypt, the Congo and Peru.'

'Is that why you were at Avebury, Dan?' enquired Linda.

'I was looking for something special,' answered Dan. 'But not that at that particular time. I was curious about the White Horses and place names like "World's End".'

Harry then asked while he had the chance, 'What happens if one of your booster buoys closes down for any reason, and someone is actually travelling at that particular time?' The Master replied, 'There is a large safety margin allowed for this technology. This has a top priority rating, as without this we are marooned, so to speak. Everything stops, if serious enough to get back on line. But don't concern yourself, the minimum is one buoy for every five light years, so you see – the safety margin is well looked after.'

Then The Master came out with a question. 'Now that we have come to know each other a little better, I would like you two to call me Voss ... Also, how would you two, accompanied by Dan of course, like to visit Anthena?' Surprised at the offer presented to them, even though he had briefly mentioned it earlier. Harry spoke for both of them. Linda looked at him. Here we go again, she said to herself confirming her fears. I knew it!

'We would love to ... It would be an honour to visit your home world, but these surprises we keep getting...'

'That is normal, this experience you are having is all new to you. I would feel the same. There is nothing to worry about, I assure you. I let you know as soon as it is arranged, because I have a story to tell you about our home world. I'll discuss this with you later.'

Sarah met them as they were leaving. 'Sorry,' she said, 'but I do have to escort you to your quarters, it's regulations.'

Inside their quarters, Sarah showed them the two key buttons on the room control computer for their inducement while they slept. Sarah also informed them that the computers monitored everybody on board – where they were, sleeping or working, or if unwell – purely for security.

'This inducement is optional,' said Sarah, 'press that key for no, and that for yes. I have set the key for yes, so if you do want the inducement, there is no need for you to do anything. Don't forget, the computer is voice-activated for anything else you need.'

As Sarah went to the door to leave, 'Oh,' she said, with a cheeky smile, 'I nearly forgot to give you an important tip. If lying down with your head on the pillow, and you want to talk, leave the light on. Then turn the light off when you want to sleep. See you in the morning ... Good night.'

Linda and Harry were ready for bed; it had been another long day. After a few minutes and talking about the events of the day, they jumped into bed then cuddled down to each other.

Harry spoke an order, 'Computer, dim lights.' After a few moments, Linda commented on Sarah's tip, then she clicked and said seductively, 'Harry ... I think you'd better leave that light on ...'

5

By looking at the time, they awoke to morning in space. Both of them had had a good refreshing sleep, although they did not feel any wiser from the so-called overnight inducement treatment.

Sarah brought them breakfast.

In the conversation during breakfast, Sarah informed them that the preliminary trip to Anthena would be this morning. She apologised for these quick tours. 'At a later date you will be able to visit at your leisure. It wasn't meant to be this way. The plan was for you both to spend a few days here, but at the moment there is something big brewing; I don't know the details yet. The rush is for you both to have a general picture now, in case there's no time later.' For some reason, both Linda and Harry felt good about the forthcoming trip and the understanding of the present situation.

At The Master's operation suite, they met Lesley, who would be accompanying them on their trip. A few minutes later, Dan and the cloaked Voss came into the office. Voss enquired if they had slept well, and if the inducement they had received was working. 'You won't feel any effects from this treatment until a subject matter concerning our race comes up, then you will realise how informative the inducement has been for you. Don't fight it. Just let it work for you, relax and accept the thoughts that are conveyed in your mind.'

A short while later, the entourage made their way to the Airport Lounge. Lesley talked them through the procedures and to follow her instructions in the Lounge. At the reception area, The Master passed over his authorisation papers to the two uniformed women checking his party.

Once they were cleared, all the party received processed microchip passes. Lesley led Linda and Harry through to the departure area, keeping them in the middle of their group. They all stood in a large room that looked like two rooms that have been converted into one. In the other room, they could see two more uniformed women looking at them, with a sign behind them saying Arrivals. Then a voice loud and clear said, 'Will The Master's party please pass through to the arrivals reception area.'

The Master went through to the reception area, followed by his party. While The Master had his papers checked, he turned to the newcomers, smiled and said, 'Welcome to Anthena.'

For a second or two, they looked at each other, then Linda said in a disbelief surprised stutter, 'You mean . . . we are here on Anthena? It's . . . that simple?' Just then, it dawned on both of them that they had travelled 600 light years across space in the few moments it had taken them to walk from one room to the other, without any ill effects. The only reaction they had was accepting the reality as the truth, which soon proved itself. From this morning until now, Linda had not noticed any nervous tension within herself and consequently the butterflies she had yesterday had disappeared. She told Harry about it, and Harry replied he had noticed the same feelings. Could be something to do with the inducement treatment.

Before they left the terminal building, Voss took them to a nearby office to be away from the busy Lounge. He didn't want to discuss Anthena's predicament until they had arrived and seen for themselves. The following statement shocked

Linda and Harry. 'We have two suns, and Anthena is dying. Aeons ago our suns were on each horizon, now they are coming closer together, eventually to become one. Over the last two centuries our civilisation has moved to a new world, taking with it all its livestock plus most of all the wildlife in a "Noah's Ark" operation. Today there are only about a million essential people left here, maintaining services until we have to leave here in about fifty years.'

Outside, it was very hot and they could see the two suns above them as they boarded a single capsule carrying up to 12 people at a time. The capsules were enclosed in transparent tubes, criss-crossing the city, some a few feet above the ground, others high as tall buildings, crossing the metropolis. Lesley spoke to the onboard computer and away they went, fast and smooth, to join the other capsules of the city's intricate transport complex. Lesley answered and explained many questions from the inquisitive pair. They learned a lot from Lesley that day, matters like, no cars or pollution; you could have your own private capsule; a high percentage of the population lived in the area where they worked. Anthena was like Earth in many ways, but was three-fifths land and two-fifths water, consisting of two large oceans. Harry said he felt lighter on his feet. Lesley replied that this was due to there being slightly less gravity.

They toured the city all morning and the outskirts to the country. Unlike Earth, the city was completely different from what they had expected in their imagination of a very old civilisation.

'Sorry about the whistle-stop tour, but we have to return,' informed Voss. 'Now I hope seeing our world has helped you both to see how we live, our culture and the technology. You are welcome to return to visit here and our New World when the operation is over.'

Dan told them he was instructed not to mention that

Anthena was dying. 'Voss wanted you two to see at first hand how technology can save a civilisation.'

On their return to the mothership, Linda and Harry noticed large photographs on the corridor walls outside The Master's suite. They were not aware of them on their way out with so much on their minds. On seeing them, they stopped to have a closer look. They were pictures of various space vessels. One was globe-shaped, so Harry asked, 'Is that the one we are on now?'

Voss replied, 'Yes, and the smaller one next to that is its predecessor. All our vessels that have served here are named after Earth's famous naval captains. This ship is, oddly, named by this crew as *Lady Hamilton* because our sister ship, the *Lord Nelson*, was stationed here first, briefly, to relieve our predecessor before we arrived. She has been consort to us many times since. At the present time she is manoeuvring to be on station near Nacania. They know she is in their area. Although her shields protect her, the Nacanians have stepped up their cold war with us.

'These motherships are stationed at every world we have populated. The building of these ships take about twenty to twenty-five years, and on average they are replaced about every hundred years, maybe more, depending on their size and operational status.

'When these ships are completed and fully checked out after trials, they are sent to their operational area, be it a new colony, or as replacement to an older ship. While on passage, the maintenance crew on board shake down the whole ship on its maiden voyage for appraising operation status. The ship travels at cruising speed of one light year per day, leaving a trail of booster buoys to the new colony. This ship, for example, took about nineteen months to arrive here.'

In the security of his operation suite, Voss hesitated for a few moments, then dropped another bombshell on them. 'Now that you have had a trip to our home, and the problem-solving we had there – plus a taste of how safe and easy it is to travel – very soon, we also want you to visit Nacania and experience the differences between these two worlds.'

'WHAT?' exclaimed Linda and Harry together in liaison. Even Dan was surprised at the very idea of the trip. He knew how hostile the Nacanians could be, especially on seeing Linda from Earth.

'You will be perfectly safe, no harm will come to you,' continued Voss, his eyebrows lifting once again, as if he was the one under questioning. 'These instructions have come from above. I'm afraid there is still a bit of a kerfuffle going on at the moment. Until I receive further information for an explanation, I can't tell you anymore. If Linda wishes us to withdraw our commission then I will notify the Elders immediately; otherwise Linda has to go to Nacania. I did say in the contract there would be some bad moments. You Harry, and your father, are to support her.'

Linda turned and looked towards Harry for guidance. Dan came over to confer with them. It was very brief, Linda said to them she would go, the men nodded their support for her, then Harry gave her a loving hug. Linda went to speak to Voss. He silenced her with a simple raised gesture of his hand, he understood. He spoke instead.

'You will be put down on their world from the *Lord Nelson*. For your protection ... how can I put it ... inside a force field bubble transported down from the ship. While you are down there, you will be able to smell, hear and feel the atmosphere of their planet, as if you were open to their environment. We could make you invisible, but then you wouldn't receive the true reaction of these people. Needless to say, the duration down there will only be for thirty seconds; you won't need any more!'

'When?' asked Linda patiently, hoping she sounded determined.

Harry came up behind her and placed his hands reassuringly on her shoulders. She felt like stepping back one step into his arms for comfort.

'This afternoon,' said Voss, looking in fascination of the scene before him.

'Then you may return home this evening.'

Dan stepped forward and requested, 'I would like to accompany them to Nacania, if possible, as I, myself, have not been there.'

'I thought you might want to, Dan. Get yourselves something to eat, and be back here at two.'

Dan stayed behind for a quick chat, while Linda and Harry left. They were met by their ever-faithful Sarah to escort them to lunch at one of the several dining areas on board this colossus of a ship.

On their way, Linda asked Sarah if she could possibly join them.

'Thank you, I would love to. I've being dying to have a chat with you two. I will be with you in a second, I'll just let them know where I am.' With that, Sarah stepped aside and communicated with her superiors.

In the dining area, with Sarah ahead of them, they helped themselves. Various members of the crew were coming and going all the time and seemed to know who they were. Linda asked Sarah if this was so. 'Certainly,' she replied. 'All the crew on board are kept informed about everything. Anyway, you two are quite the celebrities, you with the commission and Harry reunited with his father.'

'You mean to say,' said Harry, lowering his voice as he spoke to Sarah, 'they know all about us.'

'Yes, of course,' she said with a knowing grin on her pretty face. 'Both of you are a news item, so they know why you are here.'

Linda went a little bit red as Harry looked around, but

nobody was taking any notice of them. When they had finished their meal, Harry went for second helpings of a tasty alien speciality they both took a liking to.

While he was away, Sarah leaned forward to speak to Linda and asked if she wanted a tip, as they were returning home that evening. Sarah felt they were on the same wavelength and thought she would appreciate what she was about to disclose to her. After Linda heard, intrigued and fascinated, she looked at Sarah and said, 'No ... surely not ... really? Please, Sarah, you have to set it up for me.'

Harry returned and sat down. He could see they had been having a girlie chat together by their expressions on their faces. There was no point in asking what women talked about, so he kept quiet. He did try to read Linda's face, but this time he had no idea as Linda was now trying to keep a straight face.

A little while later, Sarah saw them back to their room and checked the room computer. She left, saying she would be back by two.

'Ah, alone at last,' stated Harry, and came up to Linda and gave her a kiss. Then hinted, 'What shall we do for the next hour?'

'Well, I'm going to have a lie down and relax,' stated Linda, ignoring the hint. 'My mind is racing after this morning.'

'Not a bad idea, I'll join you. Unwind for a little while.' He kicked off his shoes and went over to the computer.

'That sleep switch is off,' he said as he returned and stretched out on the bed. He dimmed the lights and closed his eyes. Linda did the same and after a few moments, turned on her side and put her arm around his waist.

Harry felt her softness come closer to him. This is no good, he thought. He also turned over to face her. She was smiling at him. 'I know you like your cuddles...' He came closer and gave her a light kiss. She responded to his advances. After a few moments cuddling, Harry began to feel strange – Linda also felt the same sensation, but she was expecting it.

As they prepared themselves for Sarah's arrival, just before two Linda explained that Sarah gave her the tip about the bed. There was an anti-gravity sleeping mode for the bed only, controlled by the computer, for people who found that they could sleep better and were more relaxed in the morning, by using this method. Of course, people found a better way to use this device than to relax with, but not for its intended purpose.

'I see you made a good friend there with Sarah,' said Harry. 'Any more tricks in the bag while I'm here?'

She certainly enjoyed herself floating inches above the bed. She also surprised herself once again, with getting to know the new person inside her over the last few days or so.

'You two,' commented Harry, as they tidied themselves, 'are very naughty and mischievous girls, but I do like a woman with initiative. You certainly surprised me. I have noticed a change in you for the better over the last couple of days.'

Just after two, they went apprehensively with Sarah to The Master's operations suite as arranged. His two Lieutenants were unusually busy; Eva came over, and showed them through to the main office. 'It has started late,' she murmured patiently 'but it looks like being one of those days.' Voss was at his desk; he immediately got up and came towards them. He looked as if he had bad news to tell them.

'I'm sorry, but your trip is temporarily being postponed until the morning at the earliest. Eva checked a few minutes ago with the Airport Lounge and we are informed that they are not on line yet. I have made contact with the *Lord Nelson*. They say they are not in position for us to travel. She and her consort are having trouble with the Nacanian ships in the

96

vicinity. Please bear with us until it is safe to proceed. Again I'm sorry, delays do happen, even with our standards. Sarah will look after you. I have requested that, officially, Sarah is to be your personal chaperone. Her other duties are withdrawn while you are our guests on board. Sarah will have special passes for you two to tour the ship thoroughly with our blessing as compensation.'

Linda was in a way slightly relieved. She exchanged glances with Harry, who probably felt the same. The tour would be a bonus, to be allowed to explore this awe-inspiring ship.

'Please have dinner with me again this evening. I should have more confirmed details later tonight.' Sarah was waiting for them in the outer office. She gave them their passes, authorised by the Captain.

Sarah said, 'If you two give me a few minutes, I'll be ready to take you exploring.'

Harry then put a question to Sarah, which he had meant to bring up since they had arrived. 'May I ask, what do your duties entail on this complex ship of yours?'

'I'm in administration,' she said quietly. 'A Jack of all trades – a runabout in most cases. I get my hand in all the pies. You learn a lot that way. I've been on board over a year now. Still in training, and I enjoy it very much. You get to know all the nooks and crannies. That's a real privilege for me.'

Very nice, thought Linda, and not all pretentious about it, especially that tip earlier.

Sarah returned them to their room, and said she wouldn't be too long. Then she quickly left.

While they waited for her return, Harry commented, 'If I was early man and came across these people, I would class them as gods. Maybe they did. But in our world today, although we understand technology, we are still in the Middle Ages compared to them. We, today, obviously would not see them as gods. To learn more about them, we would have to do back engineering, to have the interpretation, and that process could take years to understand. I hope they have that intention to pass it on to us eventually. I think now is the right time for them to come forward and help us, before we go too far down the wrong road. After all they have been around for nearly twenty thousand years!'

Linda, on hearing Harry's prognostication, pondered on a thought that might help them have a clearer picture on this, the Alpha and Omega of civilisations. The matter Linda was thinking about was only mentioned briefly earlier when Dan had first made himself known to them. Linda gave Harry the question to chew on, and then they debated whether to try it out. They decided to see how Sarah would answer the question.

They didn't have to wait long; Sarah was at their door.

'We have plenty of time this afternoon,' stated Sarah, as she entered the room. 'Where would you like to start? The gardens I know are on your list, how about there?' Before they could answer, she continued with, 'I sense a problem.' She looked concerned and studied them with a searching stare into their eyes for an answer. 'Is there anything wrong? Can I help in any way?'

'That's very perceptive of you, Sarah,' replied Harry, 'It's not a problem, but more of a delicate question. We both thought for the best to ask you first, so we don't embarrass anybody, before we enquire officially. Dad is not around at the moment. That leaves you, the only person we can talk to.'

'Mmmm, I see,' her concern disappearing, 'that's what I'm here for. I'm broadminded. If I can't answer myself I will look it up for you – what is the question?'

'Well, Dad mentioned briefly about your Bible. We . . . want to know how strong an influence your Bible has on your civilisation? – to put it bluntly. Also, to help us understand, we wish to have your inducement of learning on this subject, like you gave us last night.'

Sarah was silent for a few moments, thinking over the unusual, but logical question she could not fully answer. She replied by saying, 'I cannot personally give you your request, I have to obtain permission. Only, because you are not of our world, I'll tell you now. We are not religious, but it is the core of our theodicy on our ethics, since the evolution of our civilisation. If you do have the inducement, you will see the light of our cause with a clearer understanding why we are populating this galaxy. I'm glad you have brought the matter up. After the tour, I'll pass on your request to The Master via my superior. Their decision is final, I'm afraid.'

They were both happy with her answer for the time being. They didn't want to probe too deep just yet. If they wanted Linda to understand everything in their commission for her to write, then there shouldn't be anything to hide from her. If this is true, then Harry guessed the answer would be in the affirmative.

They started their tour at the docking bays. They were there in minutes by the fast monorail. Sarah showed them in one section the six large freighter and transporter ships, and the maintenance and supply areas. The crew accommodation was on the lower decks below the docking ring. Each crew member had their own room. The guests' accommodation occupied several decks, starting just below the monitoring operational nerve centre.

At engineering, Sarah showed their passes to the Chief Engineer, whom she knew well. He explained that the power comes from the 'dark energy' of space combined with anti-matter. At the centre of the ship was a quarter-mile hollow sphere. In the centre of that was a fifty-metre ball of infinite energy. Whichever way the ball was directed the ship followed. It was safe and non-pollutant. They could observe from there the unexplainable power to motivate the ship – while in orbit, only 10 per cent of the energy was on line.

Next came 'Kew Gardens'. Here they spent an hour, strolling through what could only be called a gardener's paradise. It was a park as well, for people to take in and to relax. Seats were everywhere. On top of all that, there was life, not just insects, but birds and bees and so on from both of their worlds, sustaining a natural healthy day and night environment.

Sarah left to last the Observatory Galleries that circumferenced the upper and lower quarters of the ship. The view of Earth and the stars from there was beyond words. The Moon was just over the north eastern horizon. Harry had two or three frames left in his camera. Each of them took a photo of the other two, with Earth as a backdrop. The time was nearly six as they left the Gallery to return to their room.

Linda had to say to Sarah, 'You did not show us the Hospital.' They had earlier passed it by, on the floor near the guests' accommodation levels. She saw the sign saying, Medical Centre so she took it for granted that there was a hospital near by.

'Let's go to the Diner first, please – I'm starving – I'll then explain. Our medicine is totally different from yours.'

They were all hungry, now that Sarah had mentioned it. They didn't realise how much time and walking had been involved, even with the help of moving pavements, escalators, lifts and the monorail, in their thirst to explore this magnificent ship. Sarah piled her plate high, but Linda and Harry reluctantly had to hold back with a light snack, so not to spoil their host's dinner engagement later. They watched Sarah tuck in with envy. They forgave her for what she was unwittingly doing to them. They might be a different race, but not any different when hungry. On that point they had to smile to themselves. Linda was surprised when Harry said he was going to get a doggie bag for later. She didn't click at first, until she realised what he meant by 'for later', especially when she saw some alien cream delicacy. With that in mind, she checked her disc for further recording. When Sarah, at last, was able to speak they listened intently.

'Sorry about that,' said Sarah, looking at them, a little embarrassed by the way Linda was studying her.

'Have you a boyfriend Sarah?' enquired Linda before Sarah went into her PR explanation mode.

'Yes.'

'On board, is he?'

'Yes, he maintains computers when they report forth-coming faults.'

'Seeing him tonight?'

'Hopefully he is off duty this evening.' Linda's questioning on her love life somehow pleased Sarah. To her, it showed that their friendship was becoming more than just acquaintances, judging by their earlier chats.

'Good,' said Linda. She liked Sarah, wondering how she could keep in contact as friends. 'I'm pleased for you. I would like to meet him sometime, if possible.'

She then let Sarah proceed on the ship's medical practice of doctoring.

'Right, said Sarah, 'to your question. We don't have a hospital as such. We make use of the guestrooms for any inpatients. Of course, there is a doctor on board with two nurses on duty, with available part-time help, if needed. There is a small Medical Centre where you saw the sign, mainly for first aid for accidents. It is very well-quipped for emergencies. Anything more serious, then the patient is sent home through the Travel Gate. At home, medical science is so advanced within our race, except for vaccinations you could go through most of your life not ever seeing a doctor. There are check-ups, annually, for everyone. That way any disease is treated early. Everybody is inoculated from birth. Disease is virtually unknown, so no hospital queues. In general, most people do have the odd bad day. That is normal. Only in later life you might come across an ailment that needs treatment. This is cured ninety-nine per cent of the time. Germs are complicated things. They do fight back! Today, most unknown diseases come from other worlds. I tell you now, the planet Mars has one of the most awful diseases going. We had a colony there many centuries ago. They did not survive.'

Sarah also told them that everyone, starting at early school, was compulsorily educated about medicine. To learn and know about their bodies and especially not to take health for granted – nobody was perfect.

'The greatest breakthrough in medical science is the ability for specialist doctors in all interdisciplinary professions to step into the mind of a sick person, to access the type and where the pain, for diagnosis. Also to read the mind and intelligence, say, of the mentally sick. To give you an idea of what I mean, think of your virtual reality games: instead of looking out, you are looking within. This state of the art technology is even beyond my comprehension.

'I hope I explained that clearly for you. You have your tape, Linda. So please don't dare say can you repeat that,' said Sarah, with a cheeky smile. Harry and Linda nodded and smiled in agreement. Sarah was the perfect guide/PR. They couldn't see Voss taking on this role and having the laughs as well. So they decided not to ask any more questions. It would only complicate matters further. 'I wonder how high Sarah's IQ is,' said Linda to Harry quietly, as they returned to their quarters. They had been talking for over an hour in the Diner. Returning to their room, Linda had a quick peek at Harry's doggie bag – for later.

A little after 7.30 they made their way to Voss's suite accompanied by Dan. Sarah was off with her boyfriend, to spend the evening together.

'Well,' asked Dan, 'What do you think of the ship?'

'Incredible,' stated Harry. 'We had more time to spend this time to see how big she is on the inside, so much space. The only place we really found busy is the monorail sectors. Also we noticed everywhere, how clean and new looking she is. I gather she is getting on in years, and Sarah did a very good job on showing us around.'

'You be surprised, then, to hear,' interrupted Voss, 'she is due for decommissioning in a few months' time. She has been here over a hundred years. With the building of her, plus the travelling time, that makes her about a hundred and thirty years old – not bad for a Victorian girl. The Nineteenth Century is our favourite time in your history. The new mothership will be here in a few weeks for the change-over period and shakedown. Three other motherships have been completed or commissioned in the last three years. This ship was experimental and the only one built in this way at the time. Since then they have followed this favoured design.'

As they settled down at the table Linda asked what would happen to this ship on her return home.

'She could be used for training, or replace an older ship in position somewhere else. If for scrapping she'll be cannibalised and then sent into the sun. At the moment, I know new worlds have been discovered lately, so I think they will need every ship for the time being.'

The evening went well, with plenty of chatting on various subjects. Then Voss brought up the matter the next day.

'As you know, you will only be down there for thirty seconds, so please don't worry about it.'

While he was talking, Linda wondered about her butterflies, they seemed to be in hibernation. Must be, I'm sure, she thought, something to do with the inducement they had earlier. She did not bring the matter up. Too embarrassing. She already had enough consolation so far. She would ask Sarah, quietly, later.

'The *Lord Nelson* is now in position. She has laid over four hundred booster buoys between here and herself, so we will be able to go to her tomorrow morning. From there we put the three of you down to the surface in their main city. This is very important for you to experience this for your story, Linda, to see the difference between our worlds and theirs. I warn you now; their world will shock you. At least you will have Harry and Dan by your side. In our negotiations, we have given them every opportunity to accept our terms and help, but to no avail! Otherwise they will ruin life on other worlds. In other words, we will have to treat the infection before it spreads.'

'What do you actually plan to do?' enquired Linda.

'If the talks fail, the Elders will order us to eliminate them!'

'Have you a date for this to happen?' enquired Harry, a little perturbed. Even Linda was taken aback by The Master's stark statement.

'Are you sure there's no alternative!' stated Linda, jumping in before he could answer.

'Up to now we have tried every avenue,' replied Voss. 'No date at the present moment, but very soon. One of the reasons why you are here is to witness the outcome.'

He is beginning to look tired, thought Linda. All this must weigh heavily on his shoulders. She had learned that Voss was only the third Master to oversee this project since the start in the 1800s.

'But I do have a date for Earth,' continued Voss, trying to perk up the Proceedings. 'It is set for the first week of July.'

'That is in two weeks' time,' Harry blurted out, 'The week of America's Day of Independence!'

'Precisely,' stated Voss, 'they are our chief objective. Just watch their reaction in the following twenty-four hours, if any!' Then, changing the subject, 'Sarah tells me you want to learn about our early Bible. I agree with your reasoning. It is

104

unprecedented, so I have spoken to the Elders back home, and they have approved. Sarah has set up the inducement for you tonight...'

Lesley came over to him and said something quietly in his ear.

'I ... my apologies, I must leave. An important matter has come up. I leave you in the care of my good ladies.' Then he rushed away. Harry and Linda decided to leave as well. It had been a long day for them again. Dan stayed behind to chat to the ladies.

When they returned to their room, they felt uneasy about the death of a world. 'Linda, my love, let's try and put it to the back of our minds, and sleep on it until tomorrow. I'm sure there must be an answer.'

Harry went over to the room computer. Sarah had left a note for him with instructions.

Harry.
Sorry I could not see you in person. The programme is all set up. Just press the green flashing button, there will be a ten-minute delay as requested for the programme to start. I took the liberty to set the programme as follows in this order,

B is for bed. S is for sleep. P is for requested programme.

Press the appropriate keys if you wish to cancel. Any problems, press numbered keys 928 to speak to me.

Regards

SARAH

Sarah, that is some girl, he thought. He turned and looked longingly at Linda as she was preparing for bed.

That is some woman as well! I'm bloody knackered, I expect she is tired as well. Oh, hell, in for a penny, in for a pound. He then pressed the flashing green button. It turned to a steady green and the three programmed keys lit up. Then Harry picked up the doggie bag and placed it by the bed. Linda was now watching him with her mischievous grin. He was reading her face again. As he got into bed, he told her about the note Sarah had left about the inducement, nothing else, then they tucked into the doggie bag.

The light went off. Good, that won't be needed tonight. He took her into his arms, she went to speak, but he silenced her with his wandering lips.

After a few moments, the computer commenced its programme.

Linda whispered, 'I thought you might do that...'

6

Sarah, bringing them breakfast, awakened them. They took a few moments to gather their senses. Both were bleary eyed from a heavy sleep. Harry looked at the time. He could just about focus. The same time as yesterday and he felt he had a hangover. He glanced at Linda, her face all white. She appeared to be suffering as much as himself

'Good morning,' said Sarah, keeping a straight face. 'I'll leave the tray on the table, see you in an hour.' As she went to leave she gave them a reassuring statement. 'If; by any chance, you are feeling under the weather don't worry – this is your second night of inducement. This time you have taken in several hours of information. Your sleepiness will pass once you are up and about.'

They both went for the shower, and just stood there quietly for several minutes under the refreshing cascade of water. By the time Sarah returned they were back on form and ready to go with her. Before they left, Sarah asked them to take some pills she had brought along for them from the doctor.

'Please take them,' she said. 'They will calm you if you are feeling at all nervous about this morning although there is nothing to worry about.'

They looked at Sarah. They trusted her and accepted the advice she gave them. They were both apprehensive about this morning's bizarre trip. Linda then enquired how soon would they feel the benefit from their learning inducement.

107

'With us, within a few hours, because we are used to this educating method from childhood. But with you two it could be a few days or even a week. You have absorbed well above normal, a lot of information. The doctor tells me that until the brain has sorted it all out, the process can take a long time. All depends on the individual. We must go – The Master will be waiting for us.'

As arranged, Sarah led them straight to the Airport Lounge, where they met Dan. He said Voss would be here shortly. A few moments later Voss arrived wearing his white cloak with Eva this time, who went over to the 'Passport' control console for immediate VIP clearance. On her return to the group, she nodded to The Master who was in conversation with Linda, Harry and Dan. On her gesture, he led the way through to the transportation room.

As before, they could see their destination at the other end of the room. This time it was the *Lord Nelson*. Linda had a closer scrutiny look at the Portal they were going to walk through. Anyone who didn't know any better would have thought of it as two rooms adjoining each other, hence the danger and the tight security. All six stood before the Portal. Linda saw there wasn't any distortion or waving lines in the separation between the departure and arrivals sections. Crystal clear, yet it was about a 400-light-year interstellar step between them. She took Harry's hand, he squeezed hers, then she saw an invisible security screen barrier flash and dissolve in front of them, allowing them to pass through as clearance was authorised. Keep your eyes open, Linda said to herself. You'll learn more that way from what they don't wish to tell you, or bother to explain.

Four steps later, they were on board the *Lord Nelson*. They were met by an official in charge of the trip down to the surface of Nacania. He led the group to another sector of the Airport Lounge complex, a room containing another Portal, smaller, and of a different layout, with more technicians on view at control consoles. The others sat down, presumably to watch. Dan, Linda and Harry were taken to one side by the transportation officer in charge of their trip down to the planet's surface. He explained to them, step by step, the procedure involved. In this room, in the middle of the floor was a circular sunken floor section. Within this was a transparent, half-bubble capsule. This was the portal and the shape of the capsule would be replaced by a protective force field for them down on the surface – but open to all the elements – for 30 seconds only. That's the basics. Nothing to worry about. Linda's stomach was behaving itself, for the second time she was pleased to note.

In the next few minutes, they were handed a one-piece boiler suit with hoods to wear, so that they all looked alike and to hide that one of them was a woman; plus the fact, they were not Atlanteans but people from Earth, who, so far, barring Dan, had only travelled to the Moon and back in the early 1970s,

They walked into the bubble and were told to stand and face one way. There was nothing inside the bubble, no seats or handles to hold. No control consoles. Then they were sealed off: All they heard was, 'Are you ready?'

'YES!'

'You will be there in five seconds.'

Everybody in that room who was not involved directly in the operation, got up and came over to the security rail surrounding the capsule, to observe, take notes or just to watch.

Inside the capsule stood Linda, Harry and Dan. She hooked her arm through Harry's. Dan realised he was in the wrong position and went to Linda's left side. She looked up to him, smiled and placed her arm through his, as the view to the outside turned opaque and the watchers disappeared.

Linda held tighter to her companion's arms, appreciating Dan's earlier move to her naked side and his experience. Then a new scene appeared before them. They had materialised in a quite 'pedestrian' promenade in one of the Nacanian cities. The side of a building was up close behind them. All three looked around, on what appeared to be an upper level because they had a good view of the city before them. Below them on the lower levels, people could be seen.

Within five seconds of arriving, a nightmarish ordeal began. At ten seconds, the impact of the place came hard. Horror engulfed them. The air felt as if it was trying to crush them. The high, humid heat that came with it didn't help, yet the temperature here was normal. Fifteen seconds, it felt like a black cloud of evil presence creeping through their skin. Their minds were seeing visions of weird hallucinations. As the seconds passed, the people saw them and surrounded the group. If it weren't for the protective force field, the three felt they would have been dragged off and strung up. At 20 seconds, Harry saw Dad standing stiff like a statue, eyes bulging. The pressure inside their heads was unbearable. Linda collapsed to her knees, her arms wrapped around Harry's left thigh like a vice, with her nails burying themselves deep into his flesh. Her face was obscured from his view. If she was screaming, he could not hear. Harry's head felt like a bomb had exploded inside, with the skull containing the force. Harry looked up with unseeing eyes to his observers, knowing they could see him. Every second now felt like a minute. At 23 seconds, they were at the gates of hell! The anarchy from these people or whatever the cause was overwhelming.

Harry was losing his temper at the thought of them watching above and not bringing them back immediately. He stood straight as much as Linda would allow him to, looked to where he imagined the controller would be, and shouted 'GET US THE **** OUT OF HERE – NOW!' Raising his fist in gesture, then pointing to his throat with the flat of his hand, gesturing CUT! Then he collapsed. But nothing happened.

For the next five seconds, he could not remember anything or wished to remember. All he knew was that it was a lifetime of pain.

Then at last, they were back on board the *Lord Nelson*. Two crewmen came in to help them. They took Dan out first to an adjacent room, where a doctor and two nurses attended to him. Harry came to his senses fast. He checked Linda – she was out cold. Another crewman helped him carry her to the medical room. All was quiet in the Portal room, some people were ashen-faced, others in a state of surprise. Harry saw Sarah was red-eyed from crying and was just about composing herself. Harry was near enough recovered from the ordeal. He felt his hackles rise on recalling the sight of Dad and Linda in extreme unnecessary pain; Dad was too old and Linda was inexperienced for an Earth woman to go through that ordeal. Only because he was younger and stronger could he recover more quickly. He saw Voss, watching them with Eva by his side, looking for once undignified. As Harry approached The Master, she quickly moved away as she saw the stern look of anger on Harry's face. The Master stood his ground as Harry came up to face him eyeball to eyeball. Two security women quickly came forward to apprehend Harry, but they were stopped by The Master's gesture of hand. They stepped back and watched the outcome.

'YOU BASTARD! I KNOW YOU GAVE US SOME IDEA OF WHAT TO EXPECT, BUT THAT IS TOTALLY OUT OF ORDER. HAVE YOU ANY OTHER BRIGHT IDEAS IN THE PIPELINE? IF SO, USE ME. DO NOT PUT LINDA AND DAD IN THAT SITUATION AGAIN.' For Harry, this was totally out of character. He found himself calming down before he had finished. He had to make his opinion known. He knew Linda would not back out. He did not want to jeopardise her, so he kept it short.

'If you do … I'll make sure you'll be breathing space, through one of your windows. HAVE I MADE MYSELF CLEAR?'

111

'Crystal clear, Harry,' replied Voss, a little shaken and put out. 'Please let me apologise, and for everybody involved here. We expected some reaction from our previous experiences. We are all embarrassed by what happened here this morning. You have answered many questions for us. Some unexpected ones as well. The obvious one is that Earth and Nacania definitely do not mix. Without realising the fact, you have helped your mankind in our question of what to do with this planet. I must say again, we are deeply sorry. If you wish to take this further, please talk with the Elder from the High Lords. That man over there in the red cloak standing next to the captain.'

'I will accept your apology,' declared Harry, 'but this will take a while for us to get over what happened here today.' With that, he walked away from Voss to see if Dad and Linda had recovered. He then realised with the silence, that everybody in the room had been watching the confrontation, including Linda with Dan standing behind her from the side room. The two security women relaxed.

Harry could see his two companions were now OK, but he still asked how they were. No mention of the incident was made. At least they were smiling. Sarah, now composed, entered the room and told them they were now preparing to return to their own ship in a few minutes. Having disposed of their suits, Sarah escorted them to the main Portal room, where Voss and Eva were talking to the Elder.

Back on board the *Lady Hamilton*, Sarah asked them if they were hungry.

'Well, yes,' responded Linda, 'I'm starving. Don't know about you two,' looking at Dan and Harry.

'We only had breakfast an hour ago.' Harry interrupted. 'As a matter of fact, I think we all could do with refreshments of some kind.'

'None of you seem to realise how long we have been gone,' said Sarah. 'What time do you think it is?'

'About ten, I think,' said Linda vaguely, glancing at Dan and Harry. Dan kept quiet looking at Sarah with a knowing expression.

'Our watches are still on Earth's local time,' said Harry. He looked for the ship's time, and in a surprised tone, said to Sarah, 'What's going on, Sarah? That says 11.45.'

Sarah gave a brief reply, 'There is an explanation for the time loss, you two, but too complicated to explain now. Just accept the fact that this happens.' Harry nodded and took Linda's hand as Sarah led the way to the nearest diner.

Sarah put her finger to her ear. 'Sorry, I have to leave you. I am being called. The Master will see you later. He is arranging for you two to return home this afternoon ... I hope to see you before you go.' She then hurried off. Then Dan said he'd have to leave them as well. He wanted to have a 'quiet' word with Voss.

Linda and Harry felt much better after their meal. Before they returned to their room, Linda had a thought and out of curiosity checked her recording disc.

'Harry, the disc. I put a new one in when we left this morning. I didn't switch on until we went into that capsule, now it's run out. That's strange, I turned it off when we got back here. There should be plenty left!'

'Play it back,' said Harry. He wanted to know more – answers to certain questions were becoming hard to come by. 'Let's see what is on there.' Linda played back the disc. They heard nothing, except at the beginning when on entering the capsule. Then after that, there was nothing. Just a hissing noise. With fast forward, stopping here and there, the hissing continued up to their return from the surface. At this point they could hear voices, with Harry in the background shouting at Voss. The disc continued normally until Linda switched it off on their return here. OK ... maybe the transportation affected the disc in some way, but the unexplainable part was that the running time for the hissing was recorded for an hour. Harry told her to save that disc for a possible future study.

They returned to their quarters to find Dan waiting for them outside. He had something to tell his son. He did not have the courage before, nor had he the opportune moment to bring it up. Time was pressing. He had to tell him now, to have this worry off his chest. He let Linda enter their quarters, then caught his son's eye for a private word.

'What is it, Dad?'

'There is a very important matter I must bring up with you ... I can't leave it any longer. This bothers me very much ... and I'm hoping for your approval.'

'Come on, Dad. Spit it out!'

'Yes.' He was trying to get his words to come out. 'I think it will be better now than later...'

Harry held his silence, leaving Dan to speak in his own time. Linda was looking concerned at the two men from inside, keeping her distance but dying to know, hoping it was not anything personal to do with her relationship with Harry or the cancellation of her commission. They might have had second thoughts. Harry was now thinking along similar lines. Then Dan spoke, hesitantly.

'I would like you to meet her before you go anyway,' glancing at Linda, as she stepped forward on hearing the word 'her.'

'Her?' exclaimed Harry questionably, but with a smile coming into eyes. Linda was all ears, thinking, what's this then – a girlfriend?

'Yes,' continued Dan, his words beginning to flow. 'Her name is Kate. Twenty years ago she became my PA – still is, in fact. She was thirty when we met, an ex-nurse, and we got along fine. When Angela – Mum died, Kate was wonderful and helped me through my grief for her. The truth is, I mar-

114

ried Kate eight years ago, and we are very happy together. She is in our quarters now.'

A silent pause, then, 'Well Dad, I understand your feelings. I know you loved Mum, I have happy memories of that period, and of course, Delia talked to me about Mum and you, many a time. I am very pleased for you. We thought you were all by yourself up here. We wondered why you kept disappearing in our leisure time . . . I would very much like to meet Kate.'

Dan was relieved by Harry's response. He had meant to tell him earlier. He wasn't sure how his son's reaction would be.

'Give us a half an hour, Dad, to freshen up and change, then you can introduce us to Kate.' Dan departed relieved and happy.

Nearly 40 minutes later, Dan was leading the way to his quarters. As they entered, he called out to Kate. 'We're here.'

Kate was supposed to greet them in the main room. Instead, she came out to meet them personally.

'At last,' she said. 'I've being dying to meet you, Harry, and you Linda, when you got the story on Dan.'

Harry liked her instantly and the conversation came naturally between them! Linda was surprised to see a young at heart, very feminine person, with a nice figure for a woman in her fifties; she was a little taller than Linda. They stayed and talked for an hour before going to see Voss. As they left, Dan showed them the monitor, only temporarily installed in the last few weeks, to watch over their house. The view they had was crystal clear of the surrounding grounds. 'I see Delia has her man friend visiting,' commented Harry, on seeing a familiar car parked by Delia's side door.

The Master's administrators were busier than usual, with the bustling of people of all colours and creeds from Earth coming and going. Eva showed them through to his suite. 'Ah, there you are. Reports are coming through that Nacania is reacting to the last negotiations we had started a few days ago – if you can call them that! We are letting them sweat for a while.'

'Have we a date for Nacania?' enquired Dan.

'There is a deadline, as you know,' replied Voss, 'But only one person can give us the date, and that is the supreme head of the Elders. He is waiting on the outcome from these talks ... I can tell you, it is very soon, now that the *Lord Nelson* has joined with her consort in orbit. Anyway, that's their mission, ours is here on Earth. So let's get back to you two,' looking at Linda and Harry. 'We are making our move on Earth in just under two weeks' time. That is confirmed. There is no need for you to stay up here, so if you like to return home, you're free to do so. Relax and enjoy yourselves while you have the chance. You can return on Sunday week to prepare for observation for your story of the proceedings, when we bring the World Leaders up here for the Environment and Peace Conference.'

While Linda was packing, back in their quarters, she could hear Dan and Harry talking. She heard the odd few words of 'OK. That would be marvellous', and 'Permission' in their conversation. Then she heard Dan leave quickly. 'What was all that about?' she enquired curiously.

'Well,' replied Harry, looking pleased, 'Dad asked me if it's all right if he and Kate could spend a few days at the house. I said, Why not, it's his house as well as mine, so to speak. I think he needs that break. He has now gone to check with Voss to see if he can spare him to have the time off.'

'What a nice idea,' said Linda. 'It will do him a lot of good, especially in the company of Kate to relax with for a few days.'

Half an hour later, Dan returned with Sarah by his side. 'Looks like I have a week's holiday,' said Dan happily. 'Kate is packing now. She is overjoyed, always wanted to see the house. Sarah will take you to the docking bay. We'll catch up with you in a few minutes, Sarah wants to see you two off anyway.'

At the docking waiting area, Harry and Linda had more time to take in the scene. This time all docking bays in this section were full with various shuttles. Most of them were of the same type, but Dan's and a couple of others were different. Sarah said these were the older, exceptional models used by veterans like Dan to show their visual rank out in the field. On these ships, Harry could see names on each of the bays. He could see Dan's ship was reserved for *Compass Wanderer*, who Harry thought was appropriate to his father's character. Just then by coincidence, Sarah saw her boyfriend coming out of one of the shuttles; she quickly pointed him out to Linda and explained, 'He must be working on one of the computers on board. He is a computer technician. He tells me if the computer cannot repair the fault within "them" selves, then he and others like him are called in. When I first met him, I asked him about his job. He said this to me as a joke, since then I don't enquire anymore.' From memory she quoted: '"Here with our infinite state of the art technology the digital wireless cyberspace computerisation the computers talk to each other to allow information overlap to include other fields by automatically downloading the referential information when required. This also applies to all computers on board, and especially the control of the ship; in the unlikely event of a system failure, then I come along with my screwdriver..."'

'Oh, nice one!' laughed Linda. 'That's one way of stopping inquisitive questions.'

A few minutes later, Dan and Kate arrived on a buggy and unloaded four large holdalls. On clearance from the bay sector controller, they all boarded Dan's shuttle. Linda and Harry saw Sarah waving. Linda's eyes were welling up, she was sure Sarah's were as well.

Within moments they were on their way home. Although they hadn't been long on the mothership, Harry was looking forward to the pleasure of his garden again and decided to let Dad and Kate do just what they like – no plans! He did have one for Linda, sometime next week, if this window of opportunity held. After that, the future was uncertain for them both.

It seemed quicker returning than when they first arrived at the mothership. Harry asked Dan how was it possible to travel 50,000 miles in just minutes? Dan replied with another enlightening answer.

'We have a flightpath just outside the mothership protective screens to the Earth's atmosphere. Think of a tunnel, a wormhole if you like. You enter one end and you come out the other a couple of minutes later. That's all I know, except it's quick and easy, and man-made. I think it's a variation of the portal transportation and used only on short distances.'

Five minutes later, they arrived at their destination, stationary above the house. 'I suppose you are going to beam us down again?' enquired Linda, anticipating.

'Not this time, Linda,' replied Dan smiling. 'I'm going to "park" in that small clearing in our spinney at the rear of the garden – in there it will be out of the way and won't bother the birds.' Dan took over manually from Judi for the manoeuvre, then put her on watch, after landing. With the unloading completed, Harry and Dan carried the holdalls towards the house. It was nice again to feel the sun and hear the breeze rustle through the leaves. As they walked Linda looked back and saw nothing. All was normal with the birds going about their business. She did, though, hear a dog yapping from the gardens.

As they approached the rear of the house, they could see

Delia sitting in the shade of the garden tree, taking in the late afternoon air. She got up from the garden seat, looking around as she put a lead on the dog, as it was now getting very excited. She then saw who was causing all the rumpus.

'I wondered if it was you returning,' said Delia, then looked at Kate, waiting to be introduced.

'I've a surprise for you, Delia ... this is my wife, Kate,' stated Dan.' She is going to spend a few days with us.' He then led Delia and Kate towards the kitchen door for further conversation. Linda and Harry were surprised not to see any reaction from Delia – perhaps she knew in some way?

Linda started to play with the dog – a King Charles Cavalier. 'I didn't know Delia had a dog,' she said to Harry. 'I never saw her last time.'

'Delia usually keeps her in her flat when we have visitors. These dogs are so affectionate ...'

'Please don't confine her on my account, I love animals,' stated Linda. A few moments later Dan returned and helped to carry the bags inside, Kate and Delia chatting as if they'd known each other for years.

'What is her name?' asked Linda. 'Susie,' replied Delia, on her way to the garden. 'I got her from the rescue centre, four years ago. She is about six now.' The two women strolled around the garden with Susie, as Linda overheard Kate say to Delia, 'Dan has told me so much about you ...' Harry called Linda into the house.

Dan showed them the special disc for the computer, if needed for communications with the mothership, if and when Dan was not around. He would explain it in more detail for Delia later. Linda only heard some of Dan's instructions; she had started to have other thoughts on her mind. In Dan's presence, she said to Harry, 'I have this small problem. I hate to bring it up at this stage. I have all these tapes and notes, I simply must get all this down in some reasonable order on paper while this is all fresh in my mind. That's how I work. I'm sorry, but I will have to go home again to compile this story. If I leave tonight, I can be back by Saturday mid-day.'

Harry and Dan looked at her in silence. Both of them had forgotten about her work and realised her responsibility. They did not want her away alone with such valuable infor-mation, and of course, her safety. Harry thought quickly. He understood her situation, besides he didn't want to be sepa-rated from her for too long. But her work came first. So he said, suggesting to Linda, 'Not this time, Linda. I missed you the last time. Look, I have an idea. Do your work here; use my study and the computer. We will then leave you alone – at least that way you will get a decent meal from Delia.'

'That's nice, thank you Harry,' she stood on her toes and gave him a light kiss on his lips. 'You are a gem. That will save me a lot of time and hassle. Oh, one other thing, I need to wash and change my clothes...'

Harry cut in, 'Delia will wash them, and afterwards, when you have finished your paperwork, we will take a drive out to your place and pack a case.' With those arrangements every-body was happy. 'Right. I'll make a start tonight,' replied Linda, 'and I'll see how it goes – no interruptions please.'

'I'll ask Delia if it's possible for an early dinner,' pondered Harry. 'It will be sweet and simple tonight anyway.'

After the meal, Dan showed Kate around the house and grounds. She couldn't believe she had achieved the impos-sible, a life-long ambition to visit Earth and within a family circle as well.

Harry decided to settle down to watch the TV. Any catch-ing up to do he would leave until tomorrow. He was begin-ning to feel quite exhausted from being on the qui vive from the start until this morning's episode. Now Dad was home and they all could recuperate for a few days. At times he had felt unnerved like Linda had been, but he had to show and give support to Linda in this unprecedented turn of events.

He wondered how Linda was feeling, slaving away in the study. It would hit her when she stopped – anyway she won't be disturbed – orders! He couldn't help smiling, thinking on that particular quirk.

The time was ten when he popped in quietly with coffee and sandwiches prepared by Delia. She was listening to tapes and writing at the same time. He acknowledged a nod from her for a thank-you. On leaving, he left the door ajar. Every now and then he walked by to listen to her busy quietness. At midnight, he came in with a hot drink and biscuits. She was still in deep concentration, no sign of finishing yet. Harry wished he could help, left, and decided to go to bed.

At two in the morning he felt her slide in beside him, her arm cuddled him around his waist. At nine she was still asleep. Without disturbing her he went downstairs for a cup of Delia's tea.

For Linda that evening, she wanted to put down on record ASAP the events she had been through in the past couple of days. For she knew from past experience that time would distort facts, and she had the gut feeling that this is not the end of the line for further 'out of this world' experiences. The coming Conference she was not worried about. All that would be on record for later conferral.

Her trip to Anthena and Nacania was mind-blowing, and that was the main emphasis this evening on this enigma for her to write; as an ordinary Earth reporter to be given such an authorised VIP status into the unknown was quite bewildering.

The horrifying visit to Nacania she saw briefly, before their bodies and minds absorbed the oppressive presence of evil, showed a dark menacing environment of dismal tall buildings and long black shadows, a scary place, an impression of rats confined to an overcrowded space. On Anthena however, it was the complete opposite. Taking into account the planned exodus of the population and with nature taking over, it still gave the feeling of paradise – the suburbs of 'Sydney' effect, with the city and other towns in the distance, each one with a transparent dome enclosing the buildings of the whole metropolitan 'Roman/Greek' styled architecture within, with the system of the transport tubes leading everywhere.

Friday

A little later, Harry brought up a pot of tea for two and a bowl of cornflakes. Linda was sitting up, looking through her notebook. He stood before her with the tray in his hands; she was sitting there half-asleep, bleary-eyed, her hair ruffled and with no make-up; he thought to himself as he took her in . . . Look at the state she is in . . . and she is mine, I'm going to marry this girl.

She looked up and managed to focus on him, yawned and smiled at the same time, and said, 'Ah, that's nice, thanks darling.' Then she continued with, 'If you give me this morning, then I'll be up to date from last time. I made good progress last night . . . then it will be just ourselves.'

'You're on,' said Harry smiling, 'I hold you to that . . . I'm beginning to feel neglected.'

Linda showered and dressed. Harry had told her that Dad and Kate had gone out for the day. In the study she started her work again, hoping to finish soon. 'Linda, is there anything I can do to help?' enquired Harry. 'Yes, you can file all the papers in page order for me,' replied Linda in a strict Matron tone. 'I have numbered them, then keep quiet, please.' Oh bossy boots, Harry thought, she must have been a right little madam when she worked in an office. She doesn't mean it, just one of her traits. It's just the concentration and pressure, coming to the fore. She had changed a lot for the better since they first met. Anyway, he knew her too well now to let it worry him.

A quarter of an hour later, after sorting the papers from the floor and those hidden on the desk, he had completed her wish. Then for the next 30 minutes, he browsed through them. From what he could see, they looked very good. Until typed and proofread, her rough MS read by anybody now, would think she was writing an unbelievable humdrum fantasy sci-fi novel; he didn't know it then, but she was planing to include everything in her writings from the day they met, making two stories into one.

There was nothing else he could do to help her; forbidden to talk, he left her to it. Delia had gone shopping earlier, and he passed the time by cutting the grass and washing the car. He had to occupy himself somehow. However, near lunchtime, she was still at it. How he wanted to kiss Linda's neck while he was in the study with her. Delia had now returned with the shopping and he helped to unload her car. Harry had finished his tasks and sat in the garden alone, waiting, and thinking of Delia's latest observations.

While conversing earlier in the kitchen, Delia brought up a matter only she could see as an 'outsider'. Harry had always known Delia to be psychic in certain matters. Some are strong, others weak. She had, sort of, a 'third eye' when important influences affect people. Most of the time she kept it to herself.

Delia this time had to speak her feelings. The last time she had to speak out was to Linda when she left here after her first visit. 'Since your return,' she said, 'the influence is very strong, not only from Linda, but you as well. You both appear to be enlightened in some way. A transformation has taken place with you two.' Delia had to ask, 'Harry, what happened up there?'

He told her everything. Somehow he felt a lot better by telling her, like a great weight being lifted off his shoulders. He could always confide in Delia.

'I tell you now,' continued Delia, 'it is very strong in Linda. I know she is in her early thirties, but she is like a flower blossoming, her petals are reaching out, ready to be plucked. Most of that is down to you! You have found your father and, at the same time, Linda has entered your life, and she has found you, plus this commission to go beyond the unknown horizons of life here, and from what you have just told me – educated as well.'

'What do you mean by petals reaching out?' enquired Harry. Only Delia could get away with what she came out with next. 'I think our Linda could be pregnant!' 'My God! exclaimed Harry, grabbing a stool to sit on. 'You think … already!'

'Let's say, time will tell,' replied Delia smiling. 'If it is meant to be ...'

In the garden, Harry shielded his eyes from the sun as he looked up into the sky roughly in the direction of the mothership wondering. He closed his eyes for a while, then a shadow appeared across his face blocking out the sun. He opened his eyes and saw Linda standing before him. 'All done,' she said, looking pleased with herself. At last, he thought, and stood up.

He embraced and kissed her passionately. 'Well, I think you missed me?' she said, getting her breath back.

'No, I don't think so,' he said teasing her with a grin on his face. She gave him one of her expressive looks of knowing him too well. This time she teased by holding him tight, 'Well, if not at least I can feel you are pleased to see me – I think we have an early night tonight...'

* * *

The rest of the day was spent talking, relaxing, playing with Susie and strolling around the grounds. Late afternoon, Dan and Kate returned by taxi from the nearest town. They were planning to go to one of the main towns tomorrow so that Kate could do some serious shopping. Later, Delia prepared an early dinner for a social evening together. The evening went well with everybody relaxed and at ease. Linda, in the course of the evening, felt she could ask a couple of questions, in the form of a discussion and not as if talking shop. One question she enquired about, quoting from the TV series, was concerning their 'Prime Directive'.

Dan confirmed Linda's thoughts in his answer, 'The same rules more or less apply here. Because shuttles are always coming and going, they are not to interfere in any way. I could tell you about an incident that happened to me around three years ago. At the time I classed it as my fellow man, and I still do. But I got reprimanded for my actions. Because of the circumstances, I was told later, that they would have done the same if they were in the same position.'

'Come on, Dad,' said Harry. 'Tell us what happened. Did this become public?'

'I'm afraid it did, that's why I got reprimanded,' stated Dan reflecting.

'Oh,' said Linda, having an ear for a good story. 'You have to tell us now.'

'OK Linda, I will, but you have to promise me you won't print it in any magazines.'

Linda thought for a moment, 'OK, I promise, but I may include the story in the book if I feel it is referential. We may have heard of this in the news. Anyway, I want to hear of this incident, as part of this family.'

'All right. Since I have known you, I have come to regard you very highly.' He glanced at Kate for confirmation. She nodded in agreement.

'As I already mentioned, about three years ago, I was in the

Weddell Sea down in Antarctica. I think you will all recall this news headline ... so I won't disclose any names. So there I was en route to a place in the outback of Australia. From my point of view, I was in the right place at the right time. I picked up a Mayday signal way down in the Southern Ocean, and I was curious about a distress call in such an isolated place. So I had a nose to find out. There I found a capsized yacht being pounded by high waves. I could see that the yacht would not last long in those conditions. So I decided to help, and Judi at this point started to quote me regulations. I told her, are you going to help me or not, otherwise I go manual. She is only a computer and we have been together for some years, and in that time she has become a great companion and achieved her own personality. I have to say it was quite funny to have a computer agree and help me with this situation. We had that *entente cordiale* between us. She could have overridden my authority and proceeded on passage. I am informed unofficially by Sarah's boyfriend that this can happen between an operative and computer in a long-term working relationship. Especially when the computer is given a name. This incident confirmed that understanding between us.'

Everybody in the room looked at Kate. 'It's only a computer, he can't make love to her,' giggled Kate, looking at them a bit embarrassed.

Dan continued, smiling to himself, 'The Mayday was still transmitting, so I scanned the yacht for life. This revealed one life-sign inside, and he wasn't going to last long in those freezing waters. Now I was in a dilemma. Without revealing myself he needed help quickly, and the best I could do was to put a one-hundred-yard protective force field around him to stop the big waves pounding him mercilessly. Although this did becalm the water somewhat, it did not stop the rise and fall of the huge swells you get in those southern waters. Now it was up to him, and thankfully from the scanning I could

126

see he had managed to lift himself out of the water and into a high bunk. I boosted his Mayday signal to make sure that it was being received. Eventually, by tuning in to the Australian network I heard that a rescue ship was on its way, but would take about three days to reach him. I stayed with him, doing my best to stop him sinking and keeping the capsized yacht bow-on to the rolling waves. I could have got him out of there, but the consequences forbade that entirely. He was already world news. I left when he was pulled into the boat from the rescue ship three days later. Nobody was any the wiser, except my superiors, that is. That's it, end of story.'

Harry, Linda and Delia were stunned. They all had watched and remembered that survival epic.

'What a fantastic and unbelievable story,' gasped Linda. 'I shall have to put a D-notice on myself.'

'Well done, Dad,' said Harry. 'You did the right thing, well done.'

They all drank a toast to the, now, celebrated yachtsman.

The weekend

The evening before was a success; everyone enjoyed the social get-together. For the first time this new family circle came together with the opportunity to relax and the chance to know each other better.

Linda had plans for that night on retiring to bed, but she was so exhausted from her book earlier, that she just fell asleep, mid-sentence, in Harry's arms. In the morning, she was embarrassed and apologised to Harry in her girlie charm, to make it up to him for the lack of admission of her love last night. Harry jokingly played on this by leading her on, as he understood perfectly well how tired she was. He loved those expressions when she tried to use excuses. With subtlety he teased and seduced her. She, of course, willingly played to his game.

Today, Dan and Kate were off into town. Harry and Linda decided to join them as far as the town centre, then they went their separate ways and arranged to meet back at the car park late afternoon. Both women returned with bags from numerous shops. Both men looked at each other, as if to say, 'Well, did you enjoy your day shopping?'

In the evening all four went to Harry's pub for a meal, with Linda and Kate holding most of the conversation – luckily in a quiet corner, as Linda and Harry were learning a lot from Kate about her home world.

That night, Linda was wide-awake, for she desired to learn how she could to please and pleasure Harry personally. He taught her, on what she now recalls, to do wonderful things to him.

They were up late Sunday morning. Dan was going to take Kate to the Steam Railway Museum by taxi only a few miles away. He thought about borrowing Harry's car, although he hadn't driven for years, but he felt the risk wasn't worth it in the light of having Kate involved, if there was any kind of incident concerning the police. After the shopping trip yesterday he did have a few practice runs up and down their lane. There were no problems; it is like riding a bike or swimming, you do not forget.

Harry planned to have a relaxing day, taking in the sun in the garden. The next day Linda intended to return to her home to pack a few clothes, pick up the mail and see her friend whom she had phoned to explain she had taken a spur of the moment holiday. After lunch, Harry showed Linda a taste of the local countryside.

PART THREE

THE REVELATION

7

Monday

Linda was up early to find that it was pouring hard with rain and very windy. She was hoping to pop home as arranged. At breakfast, she asked Harry if he was still coming with her, 'Of course I am, what a silly question ... what time do you intend on going?'

'Oh, about 9.30, I've a lot to do there today.'

Dan on overhearing, said, 'Won't there be heavy traffic in this weather on a Monday morning?'

'Yes, I think it would be better if we went later,' stated Harry to Linda. 'That road can be slow at times.' Dan cut in by suggesting, 'I know, give me a chance to check the oil on the old taxi and we'll be there in a few minutes. As it is wet, Kate and I are not going to go anywhere today.' Linda didn't quite catch on to what he meant for a moment, but she still repeated 'taxi?', looking across to Dan as she clicked and understood his suggestion. At that moment the yolk portion from the soft boiled egg Linda was eating slipped off her spoon and fell inside her low-necked top and ended up in her ample cleavage. As all eyes were on her, they watched it fall in slow motion; although there was no sound, the men swore they heard it go plop. 'Oh sh ... sugar!' she said annoyed, and realising they all saw it, blushing, she got up quickly, 'Excuse me!' she said, embarrassed, as she left the table for the privacy of the bathroom. 'OK boys, put your eyeballs back in,' said Kate firmly, but couldn't help smiling at the situation.

When Linda returned, the men carried on talking as if nothing had happened, but she could see the pretence in their eyes – men! 'Well,' said Harry, turning to her, 'how about it, do you want to accept Dad's proposal?' 'Yes, I'm game,' responded Linda vaguely, wondering how do you park a shuttle in the suburbs of London. Both Harry and Dan burst out laughing and they had to leave the room to save further embarrassment to Linda. 'What's the joke?' said Linda patiently to Kate, putting her hands on her hips in an annoyed stance as the two men left hurriedly like little boys avoiding teacher.

'Don't take any notice, Linda, they've just got the giggles that's all.'

Delia came across from the kitchen, trying to keep a straight face, and commented, 'I think I heard them talking about Venus fly traps ...'

'Oh, I get it,' she stated. Men and their funny sexist portrayals of women. 'Wait until I get my hands on Harry later.' Just the thought of doing that made her feel warm inside. These regular feelings told her that all is well between them.

Half an hour passed. While the girls were in the kitchen Dan and Harry returned from the wood. 'Thanks for explaining that,' said Harry as they came through the French doors. Linda on hearing Harry, approached them and asked Dan her own question. 'Talking about explanations, can you tell me how far these people have expanded in this galaxy? Sixty worlds inhabited doesn't seem a lot compared with the size of the Milky Way, and considering their length of history in exploration ... ?'

'I think,' Dan pondered for a moment then replied, as Kate gave him a look of, oh no, not another one of his lectures, 'I will have to explain this in more detail and as simple as possible. Will you all please sit at the dining table? Harry, sit opposite me will you? Linda and Kate, take the two remaining places. Now let's imagine this round table is the

Milky Way. It is a spiral galaxy, a hundred thousand light years across. There's no life at the centre or at the most inner ring, so that leaves the outer rings leading out to where we are. Earth is roughly thirty-two thousand light years from the centre from where I am sitting near the outer ring. Now hold hands on the table and reach in towards the centre – don't lean forwards. That's it, now our hands are about one-third from the centre. We have reached in about thirty thousand light years from the outer limits of the galaxy's rim, so that's approximately the extent of their territory, barring the area where Harry is sitting and to where his hands rest. From me to reach Harry would take one of their motherships more than sixty-eight years to reach his area across the centre. Without any Earth-type worlds on the way, to use as staging posts, it's simply out of the question. I have to say they are now nearly there, going via Kate and Linda along the way. To explore the Earth we took hundreds of years, and we are still finding the unknown. The galaxy is the same, but that will take thousands of years. Anthena is where I'm sitting, and to date they have populated two other worlds entirely for themselves in the area of Kate and Linda. A fourth is planned when explored, where Harry is sitting. You say, Linda, that sixty worlds doesn't seem many, but they are still exploring and expanding until they reach the "Ultima Thule" in this galaxy. They have to take in account where worlds like Earth take time to evolve, and when they reach space travel technology, they need their own space for themselves to explore. For reasons I have told you earlier, they had to step in early. *Earth is so different from all the others.* The Nacanian world is one of the very first to be colonised; they made many mistakes in their learning curve. The cold curtain came down, and it's been like that ever since. Have I painted the picture clear enough for you, Linda?'

'You certainly have,' replied Linda. 'The jigsaw is now complete in understanding nearly everything from your explanation on this race's purposes.'

'What about the other galaxies?' enquired Harry.

'Unknown,' answered Dan, 'They never had any contact. Too big a leap to take, although I expect there has to be life there anyway.' Dan paused for a moment, contemplating whether to divulge further information; although this had nothing to do with Linda's commission, it would give them more insight to these people's advanced regime. Dan couldn't see any harm in letting Linda know. He put these words to her, 'May I add, Linda, to let you into an open secret, it is only generally known now in our circle of exploration because a long period of time has passed since its creation. This project made very big news at the time of the mission launch.' Dan paused again as Linda gave him her undivided attention.

'This may sound to be beyond your comprehension ... There is an ongoing expedition to Andromeda. This operation is enormous...'

'*Andromeda*?' repeated Linda, a little puzzled, looking to Harry for help.

Harry understood Dad's somewhat unexpected statement with his own surprised reaction. 'Good God ... how? That's a scale unheard of. Way beyond NASA's own planned journey to Mars in comparison.' He then conversed with Linda to enlighten her, 'The Andromeda galaxy is like our own Milky Way, our next-door neighbour so to speak, an impossible journey!' He saw there was no need to go further as Linda was now knowingly nodding, as she understood the enormity of such an expedition and asked with entreaty, 'Please Dan ... keep it simple. Harry will answer any queries from me later, on anything I'm not sure of.' Dan gave a little smile as he went on to explain. Good, Linda was not letting this go over the top of her head.

'This ship was built especially for this mission. She is twice as big as *Lady Hamilton* is, she started her long epic voyage well over a millennium ago. As I said before, the first exploration is always the difficult one, but with the laying of her buoys on passage – now this is the wonder of it all, ninety per cent of the ship is "mothballed", with only a skeleton crew on board accompanied by a small ongoing maintenance team. Each month, rotating crews through the buoy system are relieved. Can you imagine that happening in Captain Cook's time?'

Harry interrupted with two questions in one, 'Dad, how long is this journey going to take – she must be doing an enormous speed surely to compensate for such an immense distance involved?'

'She is travelling in a hyperspace continuum of five light years per day ... and the surprise is, which I'm looking forward to, is that she will arrive at her destination in about two years' time. Then the real exploration will begin, taking many years, using her as a homebase. Their first primary objective is to find an environmentally friendly planet...'

Linda was scribbling away on her notepad, then looked up, expecting more.

'That's it, Linda,' stated Dan, smiling at her. He had also surprised himself by cutting short his habit of lecturing. 'You wanted it short and simple. I suggest you ask the ship's computer library banks for any further details. There are subject files of information on every aspect concerning the expedition. Perhaps Harry ... you'll take the time to have a look? Sarah will help you there.'

Linda cut in by saying, 'I was never interested in sci-fi before I met Harry, but now with all the reality before me, I realise my horizons were pretty limited, even as a writer. I have watched those TV programmes, but I never gave them much serious thought. Now I'm here it's like being on your Captain Cook's ship with an extraterrestrial cold war thrown in. I've nearly wet my knickers at times not knowing what's coming next or not understanding the situation. I have said sometimes, why me? What the hell am I doing here? With

135

Harry by my side and Sarah's openness, plus your help and advice, I'd like to say I'm now glad to be here.'

Dan swallowed as he returned Linda's compliment. 'Thank you, Linda. I'd like to say they are very pleased to have chosen you. In fact, they are impressed with your attitude, your enthusiasm. Your questions tell them you are on the ball, even when at the beginning as a novice and perhaps a little sceptic. That was understandable under the circumstances of our meeting. May I add that I had the final say in choosing you for the benefit of yourself and Harry...?'

'Oh,' said Linda surprised, then looking at Harry with loving eyes, 'I'm pleased you did. Harry, as well as you, has opened my soul to life.'

Dan was pleased with her words, and with a grin stated, 'I shall look forward to reading your book just for your point of view. I hope the World Leaders next week will accept why they have been brought up here like you have.'

'Thank you, I am honoured to hear you say that,' said Linda proudly, thinking the cunning so and so now admits trying to bring us together. Harry interrupted her thoughts by asking if they were still going to her flat.

'Er, no. I've changed my mind. Do you mind if we go tomorrow instead?' looking at Dan apologetically. 'A girl can change her mind, you know,' she said with a feminine prerogative look on her face as she saw the men smiling at her.

'That's all right by me,' said Dan. 'Why the change of mind?'

'Well, it's stopped raining and I do want to buy something I saw in town for Harry.'

'Oh ... OK,' muttered Harry, surprised. He paused, then continued, 'Provided I may buy you something in exchange.'

'And what are you going to buy me, Harry?' asked Linda amused and fascinated at the same time. 'A little pressie ...'

'No,' stated Harry. 'I'd like to buy you an en ... er, a ring.' Too late, Harry had realised he had voiced his thoughts.

Damn! he thought, biting his tongue. He wanted to surprise her later.

There was total silence in the room. Even Delia stopped what she was doing in the kitchen and turned and looked with the others at Harry and Linda. A somewhat stunned audience waited for some kind of answer from Linda.

Linda's heart rate started to race.

'Is ... is that a proposal, Harry?' she blurted out. She was taken aback, her face going red and hot with her blushes. Harry had stunned himself by losing his presence of mind at the wrong moment.

Linda had learned to expect the unexpected since her arrival here two weeks ago. She had hoped that Harry would in the future, but so soon and in front of witnesses as well! Linda gathered her wits and realised Harry had goofed. I will play on it, she thought, to save further embarrassment. I won't give a definite answer and also make Harry chew over his blunder. Keeping a straight face, she replied, 'That's not very romantic, Harry. A girl expects something better than that. I want to be wooed, a candlelit table, and I want you on your knees if you are going to propose. Then ... I may give you an answer.'

Linda thought she had handled that all right. She gave them all a smile and exited stage left, thinking, ponder on that, Harry boy. Linda felt the deafening silence behind her as she left the room, her heart pounding like a drum. She went upstairs, and now alone in the bedroom punched the air with glee, saying YES! YES!

Downstairs, Dan spoke, grinning. 'Well, Linda can be quite a madam when she wants to be,' then he said quietly to Harry, 'have you done anything about it, Harry?'

'She is just a good actress at times, Dad,' muttered Harry in deep thought. 'Nothing to worry about, it's just her way when confronted. But I'm working on it. Dinner Friday evening here,' he said to everybody positively. 'Just the two of us. I'll propose to Linda then.' He went over to Delia, a little embarrassed. She knew what Harry was going to say to her.

'Leave it to me,' she said before he could speak. 'I'll prepare something special for the occasion.'

Thank you Delia, I know I can rely on you. The atmosphere would be more romantic here, and I think Linda would be expecting a restaurant night out, so I hope I can still give her a surprise.'

Harry then went looking for Linda. He found her, a little tearful, sitting on the bed. Linda knew he would come and comfort her... the surprise gone.

'I'm sorry,' he said, pulling Linda to her feet and kissing her.

'I'm sorry too. Let's forget it and go into town. I have a shopping itch.'

Shopping in town took most of the day. Linda shopped while she had the opportunity for both of them, with the emphasis on dressing Harry in the casual clothes she wanted to see him in. Harry had got a bit behind in the dress sense since his divorce, as well from his lecturing and fieldwork. He found this enjoyable, the warmth as she held up clothes to him in various shops. It had been some time now since he felt the outward love and care from a woman. Later he found an opportune moment while she was looking in a boutique to take the bags back to the car then meet her in the brasserie across the road.

Linda was still in the boutique when he returned from the jewellers. She had lost all sense of time. Because he had achieved his goal, he refrained from having a moan. Instead of going over to the brasserie, they decided to have hot dogs with all the trimmings from the hot dog stand in the square while listening to a group of musical buskers who were drawing a good crowd of people.

Back home after dinner, while Linda was engaged in conversation with Dan, Harry had a quiet word with Delia in the kitchen about arrangements for Friday evening at eight. Discretion was assured. Dan and Kate planned to make themselves scarce.

Tuesday

Next morning they awoke again to rain. Lying around the bedroom were the new clothes Linda had been modelling for Harry's approval the night before. Linda was usually tidy with her clothes and they would have been put on hangers afterwards. But after ten minutes of seeing her parading around, he had enough teasing, so he lured her towards him sitting on the bed and that became the end of her short career in bedroom catwalking.

After breakfast in the sitting room they waited for Dan's hitchhikers' lift to Linda's London flat. The rain had dispersed quickly and it looked like being a warm sunny day. Linda was discussing something with Kate. Harry was sorting through an extra batch of mail; Linda came over and sat by him and rested her head on his shoulder as he read a letter about his next assignment for the autumn. What with his lecturing commitments, he had to juggle his workload to suit everybody concerned. His diary for the winter months was usually full.

Linda was having wondering thoughts on marriage and what it would be like. Three weeks ago she was an independent career girl, thinking solely on her next article. Now she was in a quandary about her future; everything had come at her so fast. Should she say yes, if he proposed to her? He might be having second thoughts or thinking on the same lines she is having now. Once things come to light you start

139

tossing it over in your mind, the ifs and the buts of it all. Where would they live, would they live here he was a busy man and travelled a lot abroad. She got by cooking for herself, and he was used to Delia's cooking while he was home here. Delia was certainly a domestic goddess. If matters worked out, she and Delia would have to get together, watch for tips and have some lessons. Oh well, let's worry about that later, it's early days yet. Her thoughts were interrupted by Dan coming into the room.

'Right then, everybody ready?' he said enthusiastically as if he was waiting for them. At the edge of the clearing in the spinney, Dan pressed the button on his remote control and steps appeared out of thin air above their heads. Then the rest of the sphere slowly materialised as it lowered to ground level. Harry and Linda acted as if they were veterans to this marvel of science – instead of a car, it's a runabout spaceship.

Inside, all four sat down. Linda had to laugh when Dan asked for her postcode. 'Pardon?' she said mystified.

'I need it to feed into the computer to map reference the area for Judi to navigate us there,' he said straight-faced.

'Oh,' said Linda. She thought for a moment and then gave the code to him.

Computed,' said Judi immediately as Linda spoke the last letter. 'Thank you, Linda ... do you wish to proceed now, Dan?'

'Yes please, if safe on arrival hover a hundred feet above the area so Linda can point out her place.'

'Very good, ETA is five minutes ... are you and Kate enjoying your break?'

'Yes, it's good to spend a few days back here. Thank you for asking, Judi.'

Linda and Harry kept quiet, but their expressions must have been read as Kate smiled at them in amusement, but she uncannily voiced their thoughts. 'It's only a computer. At least it's not a humanoid female robot!' as she joined Dan at the forward viewer, her arm resting lovingly across his shoulders.

'Tell me,' enquired Linda, 'what would have happened if I didn't know the postcode off hand?' Dan turned from the controls and in a deadpan manner stated 'Well, I would have to put you in the crow's nest outside and you would had to direct us from up there.'

For a few seconds Linda stared blankfaced in horror at the thought of having to sit outside. Harry leaned over and whispered in her ear, '*He is pulling your leg.*' She clicked and all laughed with her. 'Well, I deserved that. You had me worried there. I thought you were serious.'

After a couple of minutes Dan beckoned Linda over to the viewer, Harry followed. They saw the Thames coming up in the distance with familiar landmarks around them, then the ship went into a dive that took their breaths away and stopped above a suburban area a few hundred yards from a main busy high street. Judi spoke, 'We have arrived at the specified coordinances as instructed. It is safe, there are no aircraft in this area.'

'How's that for a taxi service?' declared Dan. 'I suppose you want a tip as well,' joked Linda. She looked around to get her bearings and then pointed. 'There it is, that three-storey block of flats. Top flat on the drive side.' Dan gave instructions to Judi and the ship stationed herself twenty-five feet above the building. 'Are you sure nobody can see us?' asked Linda, concerned. 'This is London, you know.'

'No different here than the country,' stated Dan. 'Anyway, Judi knows that and is on high alert for any danger. We will beam you two into your flat and do what you have to do, don't take too long though. Judi will move away if anything unusual arises and will return automatically back on station when appropriate. I will let you know if she has to.'

A minute later Harry and Linda were transported down into the flat.

'AAARGH! Oh my god. NOooo,' Dan and Kate heard Linda scream.

'Dad! Get down here quick. Linda's flat has been burgled! It looks like big trouble.' On their materialising in the front room, a devastating sight faced them. Before them the room had been turned upside down. The whole flat had been ransacked thoroughly by more than one person. The determination could be seen that they were looking for something in particular. The furniture was turned over, broken open where locked. The damage was beyond repair, the carpets pulled up and the bedroom contents completely slashed or ripped apart. Everything was unrecognisable.

Seconds later Dan appeared before them and was noticeably shocked at the chaotic shambles. Linda's face was buried into Harry's chest, sobbing her heart out.

'Linda,' shouted Dan. 'You've got to try and check to see if anything important is missing. We've got to know.' He gestured to Harry to help her. Both men realised this was no ordinary break-in. Dan checked the windows and doors, all were locked, no signs of any forced entry, confirming Dan's suspicions.

Linda was calming down; she now also was realising this was to do with Dan and her home was destroyed by being involved. She was beginning to lose her temper. Dan called Kate down to help handle and to try to comfort Linda. For Dan this was a deja-vu situation, with Linda being the cause and their blame for her predicament. While Kate was helping Linda, Dan told Harry that he was sure this was the work of the Nacanians.

Dan asked Linda where she kept her computer. She showed them a box workroom. All the equipment was on the floor and the actual computer was missing, along with all her disc files.

'Linda, have you any paperwork, documents, anything to connect you to me?' questioned Dan, determined to eliminate any information the Nacanians may have found.

'No, nothing except the feature on you, and that has been sent off to the publishers before I met you. My copy is in my bag at Harry's along with all my notes and tapes on this new story.'

'So,' stated Dan to clarify, 'all there is on me in that computer they have taken is the first feature?'

'Yes,' answered Linda, nodding her head definitely.

'Right. I'll check your copy when we get back home,' replied Dan. 'You won't be coming back here, so salvage any clothes with any private and personal things. We are leaving in a few minutes. There will be a clean-up team here later, they will empty the flat and destroy everything after checking for DNA.'

Half an hour later, they were back at Harry's, a message sent to the mothership via Judi on the return trip. While the girls helped Linda out upstairs, Dan and Harry checked out the story on Linda's disc. This was OK, just a normal feature for publication as Harry had stated earlier.

Upstairs, Linda thought she was all right. She had to sit on the bed as everything that happened swept over her. Kate and Delia saw the symptoms as they bundled all the worth saving clothes for washing. Kate went over and sat by her on the bed. She knew Linda and Harry had had the first inducement session, which covered many adapted subjects for Earth humans in their history lesson for their own beneficial awareness, including medicine. Now was the time to test that fact on the subconscious mind. The brain by now should have had the time to accept and absorb such treatment.

Kate spoke quietly, 'Let that stress energy flow through you, allow it to escape. Don't bottle all that emotion, flow with the stress.' Linda cuddled up to Kate with Kate's arm around her. Kate continued, 'Relax. Dan will make sure you will be compensated for your losses. Do you want us to leave you to rest on the bed for a little while?' If it was working, the subconscious mind should have started obeying. Had this been bereavement, Linda would've been referred to the professionals.

'No ... I don't know why, but I feel all right now. Where is Harry...? I want to be with him.'

'Downstairs with Dan, talking direct to The Master via Judi. Everything is being taken care of.'

'I'll join them. I want to keep up to speed even more now.'

Kate wanted to add a compliment. She wasn't sure if this was the right time, but she had to tell Linda. 'How can I put this to you...' She looked straight into Linda's eyes. 'You are with us now. In the right environment, certain people thrive. They are what we call "Naturals." I tell you now, although you may not believe this. You are flourishing!'

Linda understood immediately. She would always remember those words Kate said of her. Everybody else knew this except herself. Now these few enlightening words gave her the strength she needed, along with Harry's support.

8

The three women joined the men in the study. Dan had just finished talking to Voss. Harry went over to Linda and was surprised to see her so calm. The look from the girls told him that all seemed well. Nevertheless he would keep a close watch on Linda. Shock reaction can come in many forms.

Dan spoke to them all. 'I have to return to the mothership. I'll only be gone a few hours. Kate, will you stay on here, please?' Kate followed him out to see him off and to have a 'quiet' word about Linda's affairs.

The rest of the afternoon Kate helped Delia in the kitchen, while Harry and Linda walked in the gardens explaining Dan's suspicions of the Nacanians and the possible consequences. Later Linda went for a shower and wrote some notes down, as well as using the new disc recorder while details were fresh in her mind. After that she had a lie-down with Harry on the bed, and a few minutes later fell asleep in his arms.

At seven Dan returned. As it was near dinnertime he asked them all to sit early at the table so that Delia could hear the news as well. With the disc running, Linda sat next to Dan, her hand held by Harry under the table, a gentle reassuring squeeze now and then, indicating he was by her side.

Dan looked at them all with a serious expression. 'First of all, I would like to say, Linda, that your feature on me is OK. No information for them to act on there. Also I enjoyed reading the article. It is very good. You will also be compensated for your flat.'

'Thank you,' said Linda, appreciatively.

Harry interrupted and spoke to her, concerned. 'I think you ought to sell the flat; if so, you can stay here for the duration. If you wish, I'll put the matter into the hands of my solicitors.' Linda nodded, pleased with the help.

'Second point,' continued Dan, 'we may have a leak or they are reading our codes, which is unlikely, for them to know about Linda. Anyway, there is now a full security alert. A closer watch on us is in operation, and the shuttle is parked above the house as before. Now the main news ... don't ask me for any personal comments, please ... they have eliminated the Nacanian race!'

'When?' jumped in Harry. Linda and Harry didn't think they would go to such deadly extremes. Termination of an actual race shocked them both. Surely there was another way of sorting out this problem.

'On Sunday,' replied Dan. 'They killed or wounded over half of the negotiation envoy committee before they could get them out. The Elders had decided to call it a day. Since then they have been terminating all the Nacanian ships and outposts. No quarter was given, and all that is left is probably those that are down here. Could be the very ones that had broken into Linda's flat. They are still checking, they know there are several of their ships on missions around the Earth. We will know more later, as the reports come in.'

'How are they tracing these survivors?' enquired Harry. 'By their DNA,' answered Dan. 'They are scanning the Earth as she rotates. Some have been rounded up already. Now the bad news ... for us.'

'What now? There can't be more!' exclaimed Linda.

'I'm afraid so, Linda,' stated Dan, as he saw the look on the others' faces waiting for his explanation – even Delia, who was listening as she kept an eye on her cooking, came over slowly to the table and faced him. He could see the fear building in her knowing eyes. He reached out his hand to her; she stepped around to him and placed her hand into his. Harry and Linda saw the body-talk unfold before them, as Kate did as well; understanding Delia's long close friendship with him; she grasped Dan's other offering hand. 'And it is serious, in fact ... *apocalyptic*!'

There was total silence at the table as they watched and waited, as Dan had to pause as he struggled in apprehension to find the appropriate words. Harry placed his arm around Linda's shoulders and gently squeezed her to him. She glanced quickly up to him; a cold shiver went down her spine. Wide-eyed, she slowly turned her face towards Dan, expecting the worse nightmare humanity could expect to receive. Dan croaked out these words:

'When the remnants of the negotiating party were pulled out, the process of oblivion of their civilisation was ordered. The Nacanians, on seeing their people die before their eyes, threatened reprisal by destroying Earth, They stated that these plans were laid down when the Atlanteans started to police them many aeons ago. Their last words were "World's end is nigh" as their own world perished. The Elders obviously have to take this seriously. All stops have been pulled out to search all history records on the surveillance, and policing carried out to see if there is any truth in their threat. All survivors are to be taken alive at all costs for interrogation and their locations checked out. This is all we have to go on at the present time. Extra security teams and specialists are coming through the Travel Gate to help at this end. I tell you now, there's a lot of chaos going on at the moment, to put it mildly.'

Everybody was pondering with their thoughts while waiting for someone to state the first question to the dilemma.

'Dad,' said Harry vaguely, 'I'm thinking aloud here. It's a long shot. I studied your maps many years ago and in the recent days. That one of the southern half of England, do you remember? The one that you said you had problems with and gave up on as a waste of time.'

'Er ... yes,' said Dan, thinking back all those years ago. 'I think I know the one you mean. I have to refresh my memory though ... what are you trying to say?'

'Well, you said "world's end" – are those the exact words stated in their final message?' queried Harry.

'Yes, those very words,' replied Dan, looking at his son puzzled, then his eyes opened up as he recalled that particular map clearly. 'Don't tell me you've still got that? I thought I threw that one out... it's all coming back now; you mean the one with all those straight lines and circles I had drawn across?'

'Yes, that's the one. Right, I have a hunch; it might not lead to anything. But it is worth a try, we have to do something!' stressed Harry.

In the study that evening, Harry went through several rolled-up maps, found the one he was looking for and passed it over to Dan to refresh his memory. They cleared the desk for the map to be laid out. Dan studied what he had drawn over 30 years ago for a few minutes.

'This is the one I thought was a red herring. Just a silly idea I had at that time. Now I see what you are getting at, Harry.'

'I don't know how many survivors they are picking up from their scanning,' said Harry. 'But if any of them are or were within this area recently or show up in their history records with more activity than normal, then I would say go for a closer look.'

'Good idea,' said Dan, rubbing his chin in concentration. 'From what you say, this is the only clue we have. The researchers may come up with something completely different and we will be barking up the wrong tree, wasting time in the process. This map had me stumped then and at the moment still does, unless we find another clue. I'll speak to Voss from the shuttle. I have a direct contact from there.'

He left with Kate accompanying him. Harry returned to study the lines and circles. It had been some time himself since he last seriously studied this map. Then he explained to Linda and Delia the layout. Perhaps with fresh eyes they might see something missed in the jigsaw.

He told them that there were seven place names in England called 'World's End.' Five were outside London and two were inside the five near London. Dan had years ago out of curiosity joined them all up with straight lines and got an unusual picture of London walled in/surrounded by these names. He had added these lines after he played around with Avebury and the surrounding White Horses on the same map. These also were linked up with straight lines, plus circles radiating out from the Stone Circle. Dan did not class these lines as ley lines. Looking at the map there were two clear separate pictures or diagrams, depending how you saw them. Despite the many theories on the White Horses of myths and legends, Dan always classed them as protective sentries to the Stone Circle, and looking at the map, World's End was the opposite, covering a large area with London in the middle. Although they were totally separate diagrams, points of reference connected them together, plus the big known ley line from Cornwall going through Glastonbury and Avebury, ending up in Norfolk. Dan thought it was too much of a coincidence to leave alone. This line also passed by one of the two inside 'World's End' near London and the 'Mandelbrot Set' found in a cornfield in the summer of 1991 near Duxford by the Cambridge/Essex boundary. This Harry entered on the map when he came aware of the crop circles in the newspapers at that time. From then until a few days ago he hadn't touched them.

Delia understood Dan more than anyone and stated that

Dan spent months pondering and trying to calculate if all this meant anything. He nearly threw the map away with the frustration, and in the end decided that it was a wild goose chase and filed the map away with the others.

Dan and Kate returned about an hour later with more depressing news. 'But first to transmit the map details to Voss and he will pass it on to the specialists for them to study; all options are open at the moment. The bad news is that all the Nacanians so far captured have committed suicide. The latest was two groups of four, one group in Mexico and the other in South America. I don't know if this is a coincidence, but another group of six DNAs has been located from somewhere in the London area. It's my personal guess that this is the group who broke into Linda's flat.' At this point Dan stopped talking. They all could see he had more to say and Kate looked concerned.

'What is it, Dad?' asked Harry, fearing more bad news. 'You are holding back something ... tell us!' With a nudge from Kate, Dan spoke. 'This latest group, we are tracking them and ... they are slowly coming our way. It is getting dusk now, and they travel mostly at night because they don't have the complete stealth technology of invisibility, we made sure of that. My instructions are to lock all doors and windows, and to keep to one room, here in the study is best. Help is on the way ... so there is nothing to worry about.' That last line wasn't very convincing; they all could see that. This was big trouble with a capital T.

'Why are they coming here?' asked Harry. It felt like a stupid question, but he wanted to know the whole truth.

'Let's secure this house first, Harry, there isn't much time. I will tell you later. You girls lock the upstairs windows, Harry and myself will check the ground floor.'

With that they all dashed off and within two minutes

were back in the study. 'OK, girls. Get in that corner by the filing cabinet and stay there! Harry, barricade the window and I'll see to the door.' The girls ignored the order; no rebuff came as they helped the men to move the furniture; then they went to the corner without any further prompting from the men.

'Have you still got my twelve-bore, Harry?' asked Dan.

'Yes, and I still have that twenty-two of yours as well. They are in that small cupboard of yours behind you.' Harry unlocked the walled cupboard and took out the weapons. 'I hope they still work,' muttered Dan as they quickly checked them. Then he whispered to Harry, 'No time now, but between you and me I think they are after Linda...!' This confirmed Harry's suspicions as he looked back at the women huddled in the corner, now looking terrified; not just Linda, Harry thought to himself. They will take us all out unless the Seventh Cavalry arrive in time.

Several minutes went by, waiting silently as the light from the sunset faded to the west through the study window, then Harry's computer started bleeping.

Dan answered the call.

'Good evening, professor,' spoke the voice from the computer. 'Captain Hornblower here,' using his adopted Earth name. 'Rather appropriate now, don't you think, after all that Mickey-taking I had when I joined the ship as Head of Security all those years ago.'

'Hello, Dave,' replied Dan ignoring the sarcasm with a grin, remembering he had started the teasing when Dave saw the name on Dan's shuttle. Dave said it should be the *Defiant* because Dan had a bit of a reputation as being rebellious from his erudition in the early years here.

'What's the status?'

'We are right above you, Dan. I had to move your shuttle to a safe distance; it was in the way. I have a thirty-man team with me. They are "beaming" down in positions around the house; if you do hear them, it's us, so don't go shooting at shadows. My priorities are for your safety and to capture these characters alive at all costs. As far as we know they are the only Nacanian survivors left. If you give us space in your room, five of my team will beam in. Do you understand the situation, Dan?'

'Yes, I'm afraid we do. You're clear to come down.' Harry and Dan moved and stood by the study window. A few seconds later five security personnel appeared before them in the fading twilight. They were all women dressed in dark cat suits with various items of equipment about their body. The headgear appeared to be dark baseball-style caps with the girl's long hair tied in a tail through the hole in the caps. Two blondes, two auburn-haired and one brunette, all armed with small sidearms attached to their belts. Harry remembered the blondes on the *Lord Nelson* when he had a go at Voss.

'Harry!' said Linda in a low sharp voice. 'Your mouth is open.'

The women took up positions by the window and the door. The brunette stood by the filing cabinet. Then Dave materialised and took in the situation quickly before speaking to Dan and Harry. He was also donning a cap.

'What's this – the Alamo?' asked Dave jokingly, trying to ease the tension. He could cut it with a knife.

'Is that all they have for protection,' said Harry, looking at the five security women.

'Yes,' said Dave abruptly. 'Want to take them on? If it helps, there are twenty-five men outside for the main task of the operation.' Harry just nodded. He seemed to have stepped on a sore point with Dave, and he looked like a mean bugger. Then Dave smiled at him; he understood Harry's concern for the safety of the girls sheltering in the corner.

For the past few minutes, Delia had been getting more and more anxious; she had to interrupt Dave and asked him, 'I know it's only an animal, but is it possible to bring Susie, my dog in here?'

Dave, without a word or hesitation to ask why, turned to one of his team. 'Cathy, go with her – make it quick, there's not much time left.' The leather settee across the door was shoved to one side and Delia and her escort left for her flat. They were back in under a minute with a look of relief on Delia's face. 'Thank you,' she said to Dave as she returned to Linda and Kate in the corner with Susie in her arms.

Dan commented that the Nacanians were taking their time getting here. 'They are already here, Dan,' replied Dave. 'They have just landed in the field a hundred and fifty metres to the south. I expect they are watching and will make a move anytime now. It's nearly a new moon, so they are probably waiting for dusk. My men are under cover waiting for my instructions.'

He turned to Linda. 'Sorry, it will have to be you. Can you do me a little favour? I have a job for you.' Linda stepped forward. 'Oh, OK ... what do you want me to do?'

'I want you to go to the kitchen and look busy. Make tea, anything. I want it to look as if everything is normal and to let them know you are here. You will have two of my girls with you at your feet ... can you do that?'

'I ... I think so,' answered Linda.

'I'll do it,' offered Delia.

'No, I'm all right. I will do it,' stated Linda. Dan and Harry were looking on in silence, Dan wasn't saying anything. Harry judging that Dad trusted Dave.

Dave looked at his team, 'Jen, Ange. Go.' They slipped past the door and crouched in the kitchen. Linda followed seconds later, switched on the fluorescent light and made herself busy.

'I apologise for not telling you the plan,' said Dave. 'Now that I know where they are, I have a few seconds to bring you up to speed. I'm half listening to reports from my number two above us. He is monitoring the situation.' He put his finger to his ear, indicating all communication was through the implant. 'Twelve of the men outside will be invisible in a few moments. They are volunteers because it is highly dangerous for them without a protective shield, like the hull of a ship. The time limit is two minutes when the force field is switched on. I'm waiting for the right moment to go into action. This is a priority one operation to take them alive.' He paused for a few moments. 'Ah, they have spotted Linda and all six are making their way towards the kitchen door.' He paused again. When he spoke this time it was orders to his outside team.

'Moonlight. Moonlight. Take up position by back door. Act when ready. Force field is on. I'll repeat, the force field is now on.' He paused again. 'Jen. Ange. Tell Linda to return to the study. You two stay put and watch the conservatory door, in case they try to break through there.' He stood by the study door and watched Linda come to him from the kitchen, with Jen and Ange taking up positions to watch both back doors. Linda stepped into the study with a tray of tea they would never drink – she had forgotten to switch the kettle on.

Dan whispered to Harry, 'With that simple cap Dave can see everything going on via the ship above, just to put you in the picture. The girls can see and hear as well. It also protects the head, face and neck. All very hi-tec. I tried it out once, it's out of this world. No good explaining, you have to wear it to understand.'

Dave said, 'All six are approaching the door. My twelve guards of honour are on each side of them. They are now on the patio. One minute fifteen seconds gone.' He paused ... 'YES! We have got them.' Then he ordered 'Switch off the force field.'

Outside the study window, everybody could hear the sound of men running by. The rest of the team had been in hiding on each side of the house waiting for the capture. Now they dashed forward to ensure the Nacanians were apprehended totally. For a few brief seconds there was shouting and scuffling by the conservatory and kitchen doors, then complete silence. 'This is the only way we could take them, by complete surprise,' commented Dave. 'Otherwise they all would be dead, just like the others.'

He paused again. 'Oh ... OK ... Thanks ... it appears that one did manage to top himself. I have to leave you now to see to our prisoners. They have to be put in a secure medical confinement immediately. Sorry to leave you in a hurry, I'll speak to you later, Dan. Oh, by the way, your shuttle will be returned as soon as we leave – on alert status.' A few moments later, Dave and his five female companions had gone.

For about ten seconds everybody got their breath back as the tension disappeared. 'Well,' declared Harry, 'that was quite a learning curve. I'm going to have a drink; there's a half-full bottle of whisky in the sitting room. Anybody care to help me empty it?'

'Oh yes ... a small one for me ... yes please darling ... A double for me, Harry,' came the relieved replies. Half an hour later, Harry and Dan tidied up the study. No one ventured outside to check the patio furniture or plants, this will wait until daylight. None of them slept well that night, except Linda, who cuddled up to Harry and stated, 'Hold me, Harry, hold me tight. It's been an excruciating day!' With that, she fell exhausted into a deep sleep. Well, he thought, lightly relieved. That will help my repetitive strain injury...

Nearly an hour later, he was still wide awake, with the map occupying his mind. He decided to get up and take a sleeping pill; in the meantime he would take another look at the map until the pill took effect. After about ten minutes in the study, the door opened quietly and Delia's calming voice came into the room, 'Do you want me to make a drink?'

'Yes please, Delia. If you like, join me.' She knew Harry wanted to talk. It was about two weeks since they had had a head-to-head talk, and he needed to get the dirty water off his chest. A lot had happened since then. They talked for half an hour about various things, mainly about Linda and whether he should proceed with the dinner date on Friday.

'Definitely,' she said assuredly. 'Don't be negative, it's destiny. Anyway, Linda is committed. She has grown up in the last two weeks, so have you! Take my word for it.' Harry understood what she was saying.

'I take it I do have your blessing?' asked Harry. 'A very big yes,' stated Delia. 'You need a woman like Linda on your arm, and she likewise. Your ex-wife wasn't a patch on her in any way at all.'

Harry was surprised at her bluntness. He had never heard Delia speak so openly before about his ex-wife. He began to feel drowsy; the pill at last was taking effect.

'One more thing, Harry. You told me that both of you had the inducement. Learn how to use it! Think of the problem in hand,' she knew she was telling his sub-conscious to open up and obey his instincts – hence his first lesson, 'and the answer will make itself known. How did you think I became such an entrepreneur in cooking, I didn't know how to boil an egg when I met your father. I managed to learn the fundamentals until your father took me up there and I had the inducement along with your mother.'

'You have had the inducement, Delia?' interrupted Harry, surprised.

'Yes.'

He began to understand many things now, answers to questions, and his odd feelings lately. Now he felt relaxed and secure. He'd check out that bloody map tomorrow from a different approach with some lateral thinking, plus anything else that came to mind.

'Thanks for our chat . . . goodnight.' Harry then kissed her on the cheek.

9

Next morning, Dan went up to his shuttle, on guard above the house since Dave had left, for an up-to-date report from Voss. No results yet, he was told. He would be informed in due course.

Dan later joined Harry in the study, to put their heads together to see if they could find any further clues from the map. By lunchtime, they were still at a dead end.

By the afternoon, the day turned warm and sunny. The five of them relaxed in the garden, walking, talking, even doing a bit of weeding to pass the time. The day dragged by, still without any clues to work on. The map was laid out on the garden table in case anybody came up with any ideas. Harry now and then just stared at it while Dan kept looking at the time, hoping for a call from Voss.

After dinner, still no call from above, Dan was getting impatient and was tempted to call again. But he knew he had to wait to hear from Voss first. Linda meanwhile had the chance to revise up her notes and tapes and kept Dan occupied with a few questions. Kate helped Delia in the kitchen and watched her cook and make some home-made cakes.

In all, it was a long, boring and frustrating day.

Linda said she was having an early night, with the intention of taking away Harry's thoughts and concerns of the day and also to be in the comfort of his arms. Linda would never forget the harrowing events of the previous day, but Harry's worries were deeper than she realised. Linda was not aware that she was or could still be on a hit list. He wanted her, but the flesh wasn't quite willing enough with his concern for her, until that is, she jokingly teased him with an unintentional remark in her now rare aloof office voice. So she ended up being chased around the bedroom with just a short dressing gown on. In the end Linda received more than she bargained for.

Thursday

Linda and Harry spent the day in town shopping. Harry was too fidgety to stay at home today, and it was his idea to have lunch out and to be in a crowd for a change. Meanwhile, Dan spoke to Dave on the quiet, bypassing The Master's operation suite, for any progress on the captured Nacanians.

All Dave could tell him was that the doctors are trying to use drugs on them to make them talk, but the five survivors already had in their bodies counteract drugs to stop them giving out information.

It was a slow and dangerous process to clear this drug from their systems – too much and it would be instantly fatal; it was their back-up to the suicide drug if taken prisoner. If the doctors couldn't find an antidote, they would be dead inside a week.

Now Dan knew why he hadn't heard from Voss. He was pleased he hadn't bothered him directly at this particularly stressing time. They would just have to sit it out until he heard officially.

Harry and Linda returned late afternoon and were informed of the unofficial news. After dinner Dan and Harry had another try, this time to look objectively at the map in the study.

About an hour later Dan asked 'How is Linda?'

Fine,' said Harry, 'She enjoyed herself today. Bought a

159

load of new clothes. I ended up as the porter for her bags; for a change I didn't mind. I think she is over that episode. It's mainly seeing her flat destroyed like that and the personal violation and invasion into her life, if you know what I mean.'

'Good,' said Dan relieved. 'She is a strong woman, a lot has happened in the last two weeks for her. I think she is a courageous girl, coping with this story. It's a lot of hard work. Watch her, because stress can affect people in different ways.' Just then, The Master contacted them through the communication set-up installed in the computer and interrupted them.

'Ah, you're both there. I have some further news for you, Dan, not what you received from Dave earlier.' Dan raised his eyebrows, he was not surprised, just thinking, not much gets past Voss.

'Is Linda about?'

'No,' replied Harry. 'Do you want her?'

'Good ... er, no, it's to confirm our earlier suspicions about her...'

Harry was a little edgy concerning Linda and impatiently demanded that Voss speak. 'Come on, tell me, what is it?' A few silent seconds passed, then Voss coughed; he didn't want to upset Harry again. The confrontation with him on the *Lord Nelson* above Nacania was still fresh in his mind, so when he spoke he came across slowly.

'One of the five survivors died an hour ago. He was the first to have tests, and in his recorded delirium we were able to translate that they knew of Linda. How? I don't know ... yet. They were looking for her on Monday at her home. Their orders were to kill her ... I'm sorry, Harry, to put it to you this way. Their mission is to sabotage the conference. They got your address from her computer, and last night they were going to take out everybody found in your household after they had completed a top priority operation. After that he went incoherent, and everything is garbled before he died. Now we have got to find out what their main mission entailed. I'm coming down tomorrow; I will then answer your questions, and also bring you up to date on the situation. It's time I had an outing.' The screen then faded and went blank.

Harry sat down and lit a cigarette from the desk drawer, then looked at Dan. 'It looks like you were right with your prognosis on Tuesday evening. It's lucky she changed her mind about going home on Monday.'

'Are you going to tell her?' asked Dan.

'No, maybe when it is all over. I'll see how it goes ... until then; it's our secret ... OK?'

'Understood.'

The men decided after that to join the girls in the sitting room. Concentrating on the map that evening would just be wasting their time.

'Ah, just the man I want,' stated Linda straight out, looking at Dan, in her office tone of voice, as they walked in. 'I have a question to put to you.' Harry and Dan glanced at each other.

'With the extinction of the Nacanians on Sunday, did those who wrecked my flat, would they have known their world had been destroyed?'

Dan and Harry sat down. Dan paused with a sign before answering. He said to himself, be patient with her, she doesn't know the half of it.

'It is possible,' he replied. 'Their base ship is stationed on the far side of the Moon and definitely would have known, because they weren't taken out until after the event, and that particular ship is always in continuous contact with their home base. We monitor all their communications non-stop, although some signals do go undetected through space phenomena and their codes are always changing. I'll check that out.'

161

Then Linda came out with another question, more blunt this time with a hardening of aggravation in her voice.

'When ... um, the Elders up there destroyed their planet, how was it done? A nuclear device of some kind? You ... your friends up there may be preordained to create life in this galaxy with God's blessings, so what right do they have to take away a whole civilisation? Haven't the Atlanteans the guts to go in and face them eyeball to eyeball, or are they just wimps now after so many thousands of years and don't want to lose lives in their so-called God's battle. He gave them a test, and they have failed, miserably! Life is life, you know, Dan, no matter what form it is in!'

Harry thought Linda was being out of character with these direct questions; the tone of her questioning was of determination and valid to the point that he wanted to know the answer himself. No wonder she had the unbiased reputation of fairness plus the respect of other journalists in her field, as well as being categorised as a hard cold fish.

Dan sat there and did not blink an eyelid at her questions. Kate was utterly surprised at the sudden outburst aimed at her husband and her race. She looked to him to give an answer to dispel those awful thoughts. Inside Dan's mind he was also stunned to hear Linda's revelation from her relative point of view. Keep calm, he said to himself. I've picked a good one here. Boy is she good, even with this story.

For a few seconds, Dan stared at Linda straight in the eye, before answering quietly and calmly, so not to aggravate and make an argument out of the issue. He agreed with her entirely, but she had only been here five minutes compared with the evolution of life and of the way things are.

'Linda, they haven't destroyed the actual planet itself, nor its nature, only the people living there. We all went there, remember. We all felt that evil presence around us, they were beyond help, even from the Atlanteans. They told you they had made a mistake, and they tried to rectify that balls-up, but to no avail. For the galaxy to survive, this evil had to be stopped from spreading. Earth is the only one partly infected so far, it had to be done. They are not gods, they put them there in the first place, to populate and evolve. This is why we are holding a world conference next week.'

Linda sat there taking it all in, letting Dan speak with no interruptions, her disc recording every word. Dan decided to keep going in the explanation of infinite power for peace.

'Then how did they eliminate a civilisation, certainly not a bomb. That energy is completely way out of date. It is dangerous to use and very anti-environmental. As you know, the *Lord Nelson* is there with her consort stationed on the other side of the planet. Between them as the planet rotates, a wide-angled beam scans the surface from pole to pole. As this reaches them in the rotation, there's no escape, they die as if going to sleep. A second scan follows, vaporising all traces of the population. The third and final scan turns all buildings to dust. Nothing is left. The planet's nature is not touched: trees, animals, flowers, the birds . . . and the bees survive without harm. This world will be left to the elements for a few years to let nature do its business. Later, teams will go down for tests, and in time hopefully give the planet a clean bill of health and restart the programme to populate, but not before they find the cause of the evilness that brought this race down, and that I'm afraid is beyond me.'

Linda was looking very serious and Harry read her face: on the surface she was not happy. Still no questions from her, perhaps she had bitten off more than she could chew. Would she accept this doctrine?

Dan had one more thing to say. He didn't like her silence at all, and Harry now sat beside her, holding her free hand.

'Life is precious, Linda, but two world wars killed millions. The Nacanians would have wiped out billions to own Earth for their evil needs. In the end, the Atlanteans had no choice. Linda, you know their history now, we are sitting here, the privileged few on Earth to know of the truth, their quest to populate and then protect what they seed.'

Linda turned off her recorder, and briefly stated, 'Thank you Dan. I'm retiring to the study now, if you don't mind, I have some serious thinking to do ... goodnight Kate, Dan.'

Harry said to Dad and Kate, 'Linda has certainly got a bee in her bonnet about something. I don't think she agreed entirely with everything you said.'

'She has that right,' stated Dan relieved there was no row and concerned about Linda's opinion.

'Give it a while and let it sink in. She is doing a great job so far ... I hope you are not sleeping in the spare room tonight...'

Harry shrugged his shoulders. 'I'll tell you in the morning.'

Next morning, Harry found Linda in a quiet mood. He did not bring it up; he'd wait and see if it would pass. Linda came to bed about one in the morning after working on the computer in the study. Maybe that's why; she was pushing herself hard. When she got into bed he gave her an affectionate cuddle. Although there was no response from her, she did not push him away.

Linda was in a dilemma. This week had been awful for her, and she wanted to know the truth. For the last 36 hours she had been in conflict with herself between right and wrong, the good and the bad. Only on her own could she sort it out. She sat at the computer that evening and typed out her latest to date, and she wanted it to be right for other people to read.

Linda expected to be up the entire night wrestling with her problem and having the dreaded writer's block sitting on her shoulders. For the next half an hour she sat staring at the screen, not moving, waiting for the words to enter her head. Then slowly the odd word came with images of Harry's face before her. This has happened at the very beginning, when she first started to write her feature. This gave her strength, and she proceeded to type. As she typed away the image faded and was replaced by visions she realised came from the inducement. The picture was clear. They were told this would take time to click fully into the unconscious. The words came freely and truthfully, and the weight on her shoulders started to release its pressure.

For two hours she typed non-stop, stopping only to read and correcting previous paragraphs and making a drink when everybody had gone to bed. At half past midnight she had finished her project of clearing her mind. She printed two copies, then on this occasion deleted her evening's later work to the waste bin and beyond. She had no intention of ever rewriting what she had typed that night, or to reveal of the warning undisclosed in her papers (see epilogue). Her conscience was clear and would go along with Dan's answers until proven otherwise. Linda retired to bed in a trance and saw Harry lying asleep in a position for her to snuggle into. His hand cuddled her lower abdomen and her hand went to go on top of his. The next thing she knew was a cup of tea held before her as she awoke next morning.

Earlier that evening, when it was just Kate and Linda in the sitting room watching the TV while the men were still in the study, Linda asked a personal question.

'Kate, I have noticed since late afternoon ... you are going sort of bluish in the face. Is there anything wrong – are you feeling unwell?'

'Oh, I've forgotten all about that, I should've kept out of the sun. I hope it doesn't embarrass you?'

'No, it doesn't worry me at all. It's just that ... I'm learning all the time, and seeing you go blue I thought, is this some-thing else I don't know about?'

'Well, I am an Atlantean and our race on Anthena is naturally blue-skinned due to the strong rays of our two suns and the pigmentation of our skin. It's ... like when you sunbathe, you go red, then brown. Indoors, you start to lose it and then you go white again. That applies to us as well. I have been on the *Lady Hamilton* for some years now along with most of the crew. That's probably why you haven't noticed it before. Your sun isn't so strong and most of the blue would fade in time if I were to stay here. I will have to wear a hat tomorrow, nothing to worry about.'

'Is that why I hear the Atlanteans are described as tall and mostly fair-haired benevolent Nordics?'

'Yes, you are correct in saying that.'

'I have seen many different races on your ship and all are different from each other, but do have the common characteristics of you and me. Are the Nacanians the same?'

'No, they changed over the years and were short, thin and hairless with larger heads. Didn't you see them when you went down there?'

'No, the pain was too intense and I had to close my eyes.'

Then the conversation changed to fashions on hearing Dan and Harry talking in the hallway.

10

Friday

Before Linda and Harry went down for breakfast, Linda held Harry's hand and with her first words of the day, asked him, 'Since our inducement, Harry, have you had any odd feelings, thoughts or ... visions? Anything that is not normal ... to us.' Harry took her other hand into his. He understood what she was trying to say. Luckily, Delia had briefly explained to him the method and how to use it. With practice it would come very useful.

'No ... not visions, not yet anyway. Unexplainable thoughts of knowing knowledge in the back of my mind, some understanding of their history, life and a more all-encompassing belief system – it comes and goes. Perhaps I haven't accepted it yet. Sarah did say it varies in time with people. Don't forget they are steeped in their own culture as well as mythology far far longer than ours.'

'Thank you. That's just what I wanted to hear to assure myself that I'm not going insane.' She then explained what had happened the evening before as she worked on his computer.

'May I read it?' asked Harry.

'Yes, but later, it's in my case. Didn't you say that Voss is coming this morning. I wonder what news he is going to bring us today?'

* * *

Mid-morning, Voss arrived along with Dave and his armed all-girl Close Protection Team. Voss assured those concerned that this was customary, as he had left the ship for foreign soil. Four of Dave's security team went immediately to the four corners of the grounds of the house and discreetly patrolled their sector. The fifth stayed behind, observing from within the house.

'It's some years since I was last here,' Voss said to Harry as they entered the sitting room. On seeing Linda talking to Kate out of earshot, Voss lowered his voice to say, 'Your father informs me you have plans for this evening. I wish you the best, I hope there is a party later.'

Dan came over from talking to Dave by the window and stood beside Kate's armchair while the others, on seeing that Voss wished to start the meeting, sat down.

'I see all five of you are present,' he stated to start the meeting. 'The latest news is not good, in fact it's very bad news. Because of recent events, this is the reason why I have come down personally to speak to you all. Please try to prepare yourselves for what I am about to tell you. In the last twenty-four hours there has come information I had to hold back from you. But I think it is your right to know, although I wish I could have bypassed you all until I knew all the facts. You five are going to be the only people on this Earth to know...' He paused to let the words sink in. In that silence, Harry beckoned Delia to sit by him and Linda on the sofa. He then held out both his hands and rested them on their laps, his palms facing upwards. Mainly Linda, Harry and Delia knew somehow, although not in what form Voss was trying to emphasise. Their hands went into Harry's in preparation for the coming shock of confirmation.

'The life on this beautiful blue planet is about to die,' continued Voss. For a few seconds there was an outburst of gasps from the expectant shock, along with cries of 'When, how, why for God's sake!'

168

'Please let me continue,' said Voss, raising his voice.

'Two more of the Nacanians have not survived, but from the information obtained we have details of their latest operation. Their last orders were to arm this ... device, and they have done so ... successfully. It now seems that the threat made at the negotiation table is genuine and deadly. Knowing the Nacanians, this plan of theirs would be set for a few days hence, and in the meantime, in the chaos we will all end up our own backsides trying to find the location of this device. I'm code-naming this operation "Armageddon" because I'm afraid that's what will happen if we cannot locate the site. We have deduced that this device must be big, in England, and finally, at this moment in time we have not any idea where.'

'I think I'm going to be sick. This is implausible, surreal, it's going right over the top of my head,' cried Linda. Then looking at Harry, 'I'm going outside to take in some fresh air. Just leave me alone for a few minutes please.'

Everybody felt the same at this distressing news. Harry grabbed a bottle of whisky from the cabinet and, his hand shaking, started to pour the contents into glasses.

'You better get that map out again, Dad,' he stated. 'It's all we have to go on, if anything!'

'Is that the map you mentioned earlier?' enquired Voss. 'Since you sent the details up I haven't had any progress reports. I'll chase them up when I get back.'

'As I said before, I think it's a waste of time. I studied that map for months and found no logical explanation to a puzzle I created,' answered Dan. 'They can't report to you if there's nothing to tell you.'

'No matter, anything is worth a shot at the moment,' stated Voss, downing his drink. 'We have to return now. I want to keep on top of this business. As soon as I hear anything definite, I will call you.' He nodded to Dave, who called in his team to the patio, and within a minute Voss and his companions had departed.

Harry and the others watched them go. Linda joined Harry when she saw the security team run to the patio. The adrenaline was still running high, so for a few minutes everybody felt at a loss as what to do with themselves. Harry led Linda to the study, to speak to her quietly. He unrolled the map and placed it on an architect's drawing board by the window. Linda was now surprisingly calm, so Harry made his move. He was not exactly in the mood as planned, but he might not have another opportunity under the circumstances, so it would have to be now. He invited Linda out for dinner that evening on the excuse, which was also now true, to cheer themselves up. Linda unsuspectingly agreed to his wishes. Her eyes lit up at the thought of an evening out with Harry, away from the house and her notes. He sighed with relief that she accepted, considering the events that week.

'I'll book it for eight,' he told her. He came and stood behind her and put his arms around her waist and kissed her neck and whispered, 'Wear that little black number I saw you trying on the other day in the shop.'

For the rest of the day everybody did their own thing to keep their minds occupied. Linda on this occasion dictated on her disc the minutes of that day quietly in the garden. Dan and Kate went for a private walk after Kate helped Delia in the kitchen.

Harry watched Linda from the kitchen, thinking on how her aura of wholesome efficiency makes you flinch with shame and inadequacy with all the hard work she had put into the story. She had had her unnerving moments of tension, and she still carried on, always somehow retaining her integrity and self-respect from the recent bizarre events. When he first met Linda, she came over as a confident woman, but her dubious awareness of men showed that first day. The Linda he met that day was certainly not, on looking at her now, the same woman he was observing out there in the garden. It had been nearly a month now and the change was very noticeable – more womanly was the only word he could find, and to hold her in his arms was the most pleasurable treasure he had ever had in his life. Delia had told him he had changed as well; happier was the first word she used, considering the circumstances. Maturity was another word she used for both of them, and more importantly a third, a renaissance of life, coming to the conclusion they were made for each other. From the start they could confide about anything, leading to being mutual soul mates.

Consequently this led to deep personal and confidential secrets, even from the first week. Harry wondered how she would answer to his proposal that evening. He didn't want to dwell on that thought so he left her undisturbed in the garden and decided to have another go on this frustrating map of Dan's. This turned out to be for the rest of the afternoon. Linda later, her job completed, joined him with refreshments. Even later, Dan on his return helped Harry undecipher his original interpretations of his own puzzle. After nearly three boring and frustrating hours, they called it a day about six.

At 7.40, Harry came upstairs to see if Linda was ready. For three-quarters of an hour she had soaked in the bath, while he had a quick shower. Dan and Kate had just left discreetly for the pub meal that Harry had booked in front of Linda earlier, and Delia was on time. Harry was warming to the evening, as the time grew closer. He hoped his nervousness wasn't showing. Although Linda was running a bit late, Harry did not mind as it had kept her out of the way for the last hour and a half. All Harry had to do now was to pretend again to be impatient or they would be late for the booking. Linda said she wouldn't be two minutes ... ten minutes later, she appeared before him; 'Well, how do I look?' she asked, giving a twirl in her black dress.

'You look gorgeous, I'm a very lucky man to have you on my arm . . . now are you ready?'

'Does my bum look big in this dress?' she teased.

'I'm not going down that road,' he remarked, knowing he was being led on. 'Your dress fits you perfectly.' With that he took her by the hand, just get her out of the bedroom, to his awaiting surprise.

In the hall, Linda went to put on her light jacket. Harry came up behind her and placed his hands on her shoulders and whispered, 'You don't need that.' He steered her towards the door leading to the kitchen/diner. 'Harry . . . what are you up to?' enquired Linda puzzled. 'We will be late.'

'That's typical, coming from you,' stated Harry 'Tonight, for a change, you are on time.' He opened the door and guided her through into a darkened room. There, before her in the glow of the candles, was a table all laid out for a special evening: a white tablecloth, with chilled wine, napkins, flowers and Delia smiling, standing by the table and ready to serve dressed in a black skirt and white blouse.

'Oh, Harry. What a lovely surprise. I don't know what to say.'

'Thank Delia for the lay-out, otherwise, it would have been the pub. I thought we'd have a private romantic evening, just for the two of us.'

'Harry, this is perfect, thank you,' said Linda from her heart. She was very pleased at the thought, and was also enjoying the attention bestowed upon her.

They sat at the table, Linda a little coy. Harry poured and Delia began to serve. An hour later, Delia served the last of the three-course meal followed by coffee. Another half an hour passed before she cleared away then finally left a trolley with an ice bucket near the table, the chilled champagne covered with a cloth.

Harry and Linda were so wrapped up in their conversation

they did not hear Delia discreetly leave them on their own for the rest of the evening. Harry had thought ahead by leaving a large bouquet of flowers by Delia's door.

After ten, Harry's conversation began to dry up. With all his planning, he had expected an attack of nerves, but not embarrassment from a lack of words, especially with Linda. He had to make the move now and felt a little foolish thinking of the prospect.

She was halfway through saying to him, 'That was a wonderful meal...' when he got up from the table and went down on one knee before her and took her left hand into his, his right holding a black ring box.

'Linda my love. The love that I have is yours...'

With a cheeky grin he then went down on both knees, and proceeded to rhyme the first verse of the only poem he knew and liked many years ago. He had been rehearsing the words all week.

Linda was blushing at her man kneeling at her feet, her heart pounding at the words. She knew of the poem.

> The life that I have is all that I have
> and the life that I have is yours.
> The love that I have of the life that I have
> Is yours and yours and yours.

'I know we have only known each other for about a month. To me those four weeks are of very unusual circumstances. To continue the tradition, I'm asking for your hand in marriage ... Linda, will you marry me?

'You are an independent thirty-something woman, let me take you away from all that. Will you say yes ... Miss Bridget Jones?' Harry shook his head at that in regret, it was meant to be a joke. Linda just laughed, how right he is, she thought.

Linda slid off the chair to the floor on her knees, raised her skirt a little and placed her knee between his. Now she could look him straight in the eye. 'The answer is . . . yes, I will marry you.' She kissed him and a few moments later he opened the ring box, took out the engagement ring and slid the ring onto her finger and she saw for the first time five diamonds in a row. She flung her arms around his neck and hugged him passionately. He gently brought her to her feet so that they could embrace properly. 'Well,' he said jokingly, 'now that I have got you, I hope you are not going to be too expensive to run.'

'As long I'm not treated as a second-hand car, you'll have nothing to worry about.'

For the rest of the evening they danced and talked to slow soft music.

About eleven Dan and Kate returned, heard the music and Linda's giggling. They quietly went upstairs.

Saturday

It was a glorious start to the new day, very warm, no wind or clouds, so Delia, without any breakfasts to prepare and nobody about yet, was glad to be able to sit in the garden for a while before commencing her routine. Susie was having a wander, taking in the smells of the garden; above them there was plenty of bird chatter and activity for their young. Dan had moved his shuttle to the spinney before Voss had arrived and with the security clampdown on them removed, had decided to leave it parked there as before.

Delia was halfway through reading the book she had started last night from not being able to sleep. She had on her mind two separate thoughts of concern, Voss's talk of doomsday and Harry and Linda's future. These two conflicting dilemmas had her in tears at one in the morning. She had cancelled her usual Friday evening meet with her man-friend, and she needed a shoulder to cry on, and that would be a dilemma in itself. How could she tell

174

her close friends the truth about being an operative to Dan?

This morning, the book had suddenly gone cold on her and Susie now wanted to sit on her lap. Delia combed her ears with one eye on the drawn curtains of the upstairs bedroom windows. The flowers left at her door last night were an unexpected surprise along with a nice note of appreciation. She had noticed foremost how Harry's tower of strength, hidden until now, had come to the fore from a changed and stronger man. This alone had kept her together, to look up to him, where before he had been the son of the man she admired ...

Mid-morning she heard Kate and Dan in the kitchen, then they came out into the garden with three cups of tea.

'Where are Romeo and Juliet this morning? He's not still wooing her surely,' said Dan laughingly.

Delia looked up at the bedroom window. 'It appears they're still having a lie-in.'

'Do you know how Harry got on last night?' asked Kate.

'No. I haven't heard the official word yet,' replied Delia. 'As they are not up yet and the ring is not in the presentation box, I would say all went very well, anyway they will be about soon.' Dan detected the despondency in Delia's voice. As Kate was observing, Dan expressed with his eyes for her to leave them alone. Kate watched them for a few minutes from the kitchen window; Dan was comforting Delia and her head was now resting on his shoulder. Kate would not have tolerated this with any other woman, but Delia was different, part of the family and she knew of Dan's past.

Nearly an hour later, Delia rose from her seat; she had seen the bedroom curtains drawn back a little while back. She and Dan returned indoors to join Kate in the sitting room, hopefully to hear of their good news.

Twenty minutes went by before Harry and Linda showed their bleary-eyed faces to the patiently awaiting audience.

175

Delia thanked Harry for the flowers, and Dan, waiting to put his question for everybody's benefit, just came out with it. 'Well,' he asked, 'have you some news for us to hear? Come on son, out with it.'

'Christ, Dad. Anyone would think Linda is pregnant and I'm lined up for a shotgun wedding,' replied Harry, spluttering and yawning. 'This is the twenty-first century, not the late 1950s.'

Delia closed her eyes at his first remark.

'Yes, I would like to announce that Linda is to be my future wife, and as from last night we are engaged to marry at a date to be established later when this present so-called mess is cleared up. One question, does your Captain perform marriage ceremonies?'

Everybody came forward and offered his or her congratulations. Linda, still half-asleep, was showing off her engagement ring.

After the commotion died down, Dan stepped forward to Harry and Linda. 'Now that you two have woken up, I have two items of news for you. Voss called me at four this morning.'

'Good news I hope this time,' muttered Harry.

'A bit of each,' answered Dad. 'Our map was put through the surveillance computers and came up without any mathematical or logical equation to the reference points marked on the map, unless something is missing in the formula. The second piece of news is that the last two Nacanians have responded to the antidote drugs and are recovering well so far. These two, a male and a female, are not members of the ship's crew. They were the technicians assigned for a special operation to an underground site somewhere to the north-west of London to manually activate and oversee the systems were working properly. Apparently the system is very old and antiquated. Because of this, it is well maintained every one hundred years with frequent inspections.'

Harry stood up. 'Hang on a minute, did you say to the north-west of London' he exclaimed, now fully awake. 'Oh, my head. Delia, have you anything for a gross headache in your kitchen please, my head is splitting...' Delia left the room while Harry was in deep thought, contemplating.

'I think we are looking at this in the wrong way,' continued Harry. Everyone followed curiously as he made for the study. Delia joined them with tablets and water.

He checked the laid-out map and stared at it for a few moments, looking for something.

'Yes ... Dad, your lines connecting up all the "World's End" locations are all very neat. Let's concentrate on the five outer locations; forget the other two. If I draw a circle with a compass ... Dan picked up the only compass they had from a consortium of pencils and rulers in the small desk drawer. 'No, that's too small. I need an eight to ten inch radius at least.' stated Harry. 'Delia, have you any knitting needles? Long ones.'

Delia took up a determined stance with hands on hips. 'Yes I have, and I don't want them bent, thank you very much.' She went off quickly to fetch them. and in no time at all, returned with a selection of long needles.

The two men taped the needles to the compass with a coloured ink crayon on one needle. After a few minutes with adjustments, Harry proceeded to establish a circle on the map. After a few more attempts and further adjustments he found the centre and drew a circle that touched the outer lines. He could only reach three of the four lines. The fourth was too far to the south and also appeared to be the shortest on its own; somehow it didn't seem to matter. They all looked at what he had done. The centre point of this circle was in an area north-west of London.

'There,' stated Harry, that is as near I can get it. Allowing for a margin of error, say five miles radius, ask Voss to check out that area. The whole circle is about seventy-five miles in diameter.' He sat down holding his head in his hands. The headache had returned with a vengeance. 'Go outside and get some air,' said Delia. 'I'll make us all a cup of tea.'

'Good idea,' said Linda. 'I could do with one,' switching off her recorder which was now always hanging from her shoulder.

While Harry and Linda took in the air in the garden, Dan came out and stated that he had looked to see where the centre was placed. 'And where is it?' enquired Harry. Dan took no notice as he continued, 'The needle points in the area of Hemel Hampstead railway station. I didn't think of finding the centre of the area. In principle it's like finding the middle of a country or the furthest point inland from the sea.'

'That's why I'm a geologist and you an out-of-practice retired archaeological hobbyist ... sorry Dad, I didn't mean that. It appears that late night wine, women and song don't agree with me along with this stress of the situation.' Linda looked at Harry and in a joking tone remarked, 'Oh, I see. You class me as female entertainment, do you.'

'I don't think so,' said Dan replying to Harry. 'I think it could be your inducement clicking on in your subconscious in the last few hours. You have been working hard on a problem, and consequently it has hit you all at once. I've seen it happen before. I just hope your theory is correct.'

'If it is,' stated Harry, 'it's all down to you, your doodling over thirty years ago.'

'What made you think of a circle?' Dan asked.

'I don't know really. It's just like a jigsaw, you look for that one particular piece for ages, then you find it staring you in the face. I was concentrating on London itself, then your report north-west of London clicked. It's more central to the whole area covered by your lines. Not in London as I thought, where it is more built up. It just made sense to me, don't ask me how ... anyway, we don't know yet.'

'That I'm about to do. I'm going into the shuttle to speak to Voss and report these findings.' He waved to Kate on the patio for her to join him. Together they strolled along to the spinney.

They returned just in time for lunch. While eating, Dan explained to Harry while the others listened, 'Voss thinks you may have something important enough for him to interrupt the present surface scanning process and concentrate on that ten mile square area you proposed at full penetrating power. He will obviously let us know if there is any positive outcome. Also the two remaining survivors have improved in their well being. Only because from what I can understand, they were outsiders, technicians, and not under the influence of being addicted to the suicide drug, which all the small scouting crews are accustomed to. Also they have been told on purpose that they are now the only two people left from their civilisation. These two are now in a deep state of shock, which has loosened their tongues in fear of what will become of them now. They do not know the full purpose of their mission, but are willing to return to show on how the procedures were carried out.

'Here we have a paradox. As technicians they don't know where the location is, they were only passengers. All they can tell us is that they saw a railway line and a river close by on arrival and when they left, a large traffic system with many roads connecting to it.'

'Right,' stated Harry. 'Let's finish our meal, then Dad and I will go into the study and leave you girls to it.'

'Oh no you won't,' stated Linda. 'I'm coming in with you. Don't forget I have to record all this.' The men just raised their eyebrows. 'Women, what would we do without them,' muttered Dan with a teasing grin. Linda has only been engaged a few hours and already she is practising with her

179

little finger and thumb. 'Watch it, Harry. From now on you'll have to start collecting your Brownie points.'

During the next few minutes, the three of them studied the location after Harry double-checked he hadn't made a mistake. For their own satisfaction, they looked for the three landmarks Dad had mentioned – this could be a number of places. But Harry was placing his bet on the one that was obvious to him first. The location had a railway. The river was there; the Grand Union Canal running parallel with the track. Within about five miles to the south-east there were several main road junctions. The one that stood out was J21 connecting the M25 to the M1. Either way, all this coincided with the landmarks.

'Well,' uttered Dan. 'I personally don't think we need to inform Voss he is looking at the right location; he would have taken these landmarks into consideration. We'll have to sweat it out and wait and see if we are wrong. If we are, they will have to revert to surface scanning, and it would help to know what to look for. I don't think there is much time left, I know Voss too well.' Linda cut in and summed it all up in one sentence on behalf of Dan's diplomacy. 'What you are saying is that if we don't find this place very soon, we are dead!'

They did not have long to wait to find out. Linda wondered how long. She could feel the tension rising. She had a private bet with herself that with the ultimate state of the art technology in the science and the geological surveillance complex on the *Lady Hamilton* and the aeons they have been watching Earth won't have long before they hear an answer. She turned and looked at the computer, willing it to speak. Come on Voss, cut out all that red tape and protocol bullshit. Tell us!

180

So deep in thought, Linda shrieked and jumped back in shock and trod onto Harry's foot as the calling bleep suddenly interrupted the atmosphere of her serious daydreaming.

Dan stepped over and answered the call. Linda stood there rooted to the spot, her heart pounding.

Voss's distinctive voice came through. For once he did not sound like impending doom.

'I have good news for you. We have found an underground complex of facilities used by the Nacanians, judging by their DNA traces down there. We are preparing fully fledged specialised teams to go down to find out what we are up against. I want Linda to join them and to observe the situation for her report. These are instructions from the Elders. Um, erm ... so I guess you'd all better come up for the duration until we sort this out. When you arrive, Sarah will take Linda with Harry straight to the main loading bay to join a freighter being loaded with equipment. That will be ready to go soon, and Dan, if you wish to accompany them, then you may.'

Dan instructed everybody to pack a bag for an unforeseeable term of stay.

'I have a feeling he is holding back the full picture,' stated Harry.

'So do I,' answered Dan. 'So do I.'

11

On arrival on the *Lady Hamilton*, Sarah was waiting to greet and to escort them to the maintenance operations ship, which was waiting for them in the main loading docking area.

The mothership was very noticeably busier since their last visit. The chaos theory appeared dominant, with the ship on full alert.

Dave, who relieved Sarah of her charges, met Dan, Harry and Linda in the cargo storage area of the operations ship. Here were stacked boxes with various types of equipment and containers of all sizes being secured. Forward they could see a group of about 50 men from various specialised departments preparing for the coming trip. About a third of them were Dave's men, checking their weapons and each other's personal gadgetry. Linda and Sarah didn't have much chance to chat in the rush, the atmospheric tension and the noise as everybody went about their urgent business. They managed to hug each other before Sarah left them. 'We'll speak later.'

Dave led them to the large bridge needed to oversee the operations of a space maintenance freighter. Up here they saw briefly as they passed, four security men in a side room guarding two alien-type figures. In that brief moment, they took in a short, thin, very pale male and a female, with larger than normal heads, no hair. When they were on their world, the pain obscured taking in their form. It reminded Harry of the Mekon in the Dan Dare comic. 'Those are the two Nacanian survivors,' informed Dave, and as they passed another room, he said in a low voice, 'In there are six men, they have just arrived from Anthena. Two top scientists and four specialist technicians covering all sorts of complicated techniques in computer, electrical and engineering devices.'

Dan and Harry glanced at each other. Dan then asked Dave quietly, 'Dave, Delia has been brought up here as well; why?' Dave looked a little uncomfortable, 'I take it Voss hasn't told you yet ... all I know at the moment is that all operatives are being recalled, just a precautionary safety measure. They are being sent on to Anthena hopefully only temporary.'

'Thanks Dave.'

At the far end of the bridge they could see Voss talking with Lesley and Eva. Harry and the others also saw Dave's five all-girl Close Protection Team arrive onto the bridge. Surely Voss is not going down as well, thought Harry. This is all getting very disconcerting.

Voss dismissed his two PAs to return to his office as he saw Dave arrive before him with Dan and the others following up behind. Harry waited to see if Voss would now explain the situation. He knew Voss was a very busy man, but he didn't like being kept in the dark. If it weren't for Linda's commission, they would be completely out in the cold or possibly not even be here. But as they were, he expected Voss to keep Linda updated.

Voss invited them to a quiet corner while Dave listened with his back to Voss. He saw his team take up their security positions around the bridge. The ship was about ready to leave as the Captain and his bridge officers took to their seats for checks before manoeuvring from the docking ring.

'Sorry about the pandemonium. I am able to tell you the position now. As you know, we have found an underground complex. This has changed our thinking on the situation from the discovery of a deep mine shaft leading to another cavern, ten kilometres down. It is situated under a common not far from a town. The only way in is by "beaming" into the upper chamber a hundred metres down. This ship will have to be stationed near the common in that period, then move away to a safe distance by dawn, as we are very close to a golf course and wait until required – a matter of seconds to return into position. At the bottom chamber there is a mile-long tunnel going south to another small cavern. I must add here that this situation is far graver than we had expected. Earlier, until our two survivors talked, we were looking for a near surface storage dump of sorts with chemical and bacterial warfare components to wipe out all life on Earth. This layout of the complex has put a completely different light on this scenario. I have to tell you we are thinking along the lines of some kind of an "Earthquake" device. That's all we know until we go down and find out.

'The security troop will go down first. Depending on their findings, you, Linda, will go down with the specialist team and our two survivors. The rest of us will remain here until the specialist team report back on their needs. After that, anything is open.'

Harry spoke up, determined not to be put off. 'I take it Voss, that when you mean Linda, you meant Dad and I are to accompany her! You don't expect Linda to be completely alone with strangers six miles down there in this situation, do you?'

Voss coughed and thought for a moment, 'Err, hmm ... all right. I agree with you ... Dave, see to that, will you?' Dave smiled to himself and turned and acknowledged The Master's instruction. He would put the girls on to it. At least they were not strangers to each other, and Voss wouldn't need them in here. Dave knew his girls were dying to get into the action.

*   *   *

A few minutes later they were making their way through the mothership's perimeter defence shields. The Earth came into view, moving across the large viewer screen as the ship manoeuvred into position. At the centre of the viewer it slowed and stopped. The ship locked on, and then the image blurred as the ship went into the flight corridor at high velocity. In no time at all, they were shooting across the North Atlantic towards the Bristol Channel and slowing on approaching the site via the Oxford Plain. At the common, the weather had changed dramatically since this morning, with mist and continuous heavy drizzle. The Captain remarked that should keep the walkers away along with their dogs, whose highly sensitive and inquisitive senses could be a pain at times.

Somehow to Linda and Harry the time had ticked by fast. It was now evening, with dusk a couple of hours away. 'I'm glad you spoke up to Voss,' Linda stated quietly to Harry with appreciation. 'I wouldn't have gone otherwise. I would've refused point-blank. Thank you.'

The Captain instructed his pilot to go manual and if possible to find any-out-of-the-way hollows anywhere around the area of the common. The ship was over 80 metres in length, and precautions were required. The pilot watched the viewer screen; this showed a bright clear day, but looking out through the large oval bridge viewing windows all they could see was cloud. The pilot expertly manoeuvred the ship and positioned itself finally to the lee side of the common away from the town.

In the meantime, Dave's girl team thrilled at the change of their humdrum status on board, gathered around Linda and her companions and gave Dan and Harry one-piece protec-

185

tive overalls suits, then ushered Linda away from the prying eyes of the male crew. She changed into the suit with their help and made final adjustments to her personal radio. She could hear Harry and Dan testing theirs through her earpiece. Dave, coming up from the cargo holds, saw the kerfuffle, and inadvertently walked over to the group. One of the girls saw him coming over and stood before him with her hand out, palm up. He saw the situation and turned on his heel and retraced his steps, slightly embarrassed for stumbling onto a female domain. It is understandable, for the women had nowhere to go with all the men on board occupying every nook and cranny in amongst the cargo. One of the bridge crew joked out loud from their observations, 'We know you are the Chief, Dave, but you're pushing your authority there.'

Down in the hold, all was ready. Two security men wearing respirators with powerful torches were on the cargo teleporter platform, waiting to beam into the upper chamber. The Captain gave the all clear and they were gone. A couple of minutes went by before they reported back. It was safe to proceed, but the air was very stale, and they were unable to find power for the lights. The captain ordered the two Nacanians with two guards to go down to switch on the power they said was there. The next group to go down stood on the Tele-porter, the specialist team along with Harry, Dan and Linda. The nine beam down on clearance followed swiftly by Dave and his female team.

Linda found herself in a well-lit circular cavern roughly 30 metres in diameter. Before her were twenty people inspecting with a general wandering around in the rubbish: boxes, tools and other paraphernalia left over from the years of building and the consequent inspections. The air was beginning to freshen up, but the strong musty smell still lingered and was very wet, with water dripping from the curvature ceiling and walls. The two Nacanians with their guards were standing by what appeared to be the top of the mineshaft with two enclosed cages. The technicians started to question the two survivors. Six more security men arrived and the order was given out to those above by Dave to hold for the time being. He continued talking with his report to the Captain.

The power was switched on to power the lifts, one large one for carrying equipment, and the smaller one enclosed for personnel. Ten security men along with Dave and the two survivors entered the larger lift and commenced their journey down. A few minutes later, Dave contacted them, saying all was well as they plunged downwards. 'Follow us down.' Harry, Dan and Linda and the specialist team entered the passenger lift. Harry mentioned that he saw no sign of cables or machinery to operate the lifts. The technician next to him nonchalantly told him, 'No, there wouldn't be. This is an anti-gravity platform.'

For Linda it wasn't funny, she hated heights, let alone being stuck in a lift with no visible means of support dropping down to oblivion in a six mile hole at 60 mph. Although she hadn't suffered from butterflies in the stomach for some while, this phobia had her knees buckling beneath her. All her strength went into her legs and trying to look calm at the same time had her clinging to Harry's arm like a vice. As they descended the lift shaft they could feel the temperature rising. By the time they reached the cavern the heat was stifling from being down so deep in the earth's crust.

Nearly seven minutes later, the door opened with signs of relief from everybody. The place was still in darkness except for the beams from the torches. There was no sign of Dave and the others.

'We'd better wait here until they return,' stated one of the technicians.

'Ah, there's no need to do that,' responded the voice of Dave as he joined them from nowhere. 'The lights will be on in a second or two. That's some drop. Our lift must be slower because we have only been here a couple of minutes.' All of a sudden the whole place was bathed in light and everybody took in the sight beholding them all.

Linda described the scene on her recorder:

'This place is more dome-shaped and carved out of the rock, circular as the above chamber and a good fifty metres in diameter. The air is warm but stale. The back of the lift shaft is about a metre away from the circular wall. This gap is filled in, making this area straight; I'm informed this is for added strength for the open base of the lifts. In front of the lift doors is a long wide platform space for handling equipment. Here lies a dismantled powered hoist crane, of which the stumps of six girders remain embedded in the concrete at the four corners of the loading area and two in the centre. Within this, there are two sunken parallel rail-tracks, like a train station. The tracks are embedded in concrete for strength, with two open flat transporter carriages side by side flush with the floor for easy movement of heavy equipment with just one seat at the far end for the driver. The wide tracks lead for about fifteen metres to the south side of the dome structure; here at this point there is a sealed circular steel door. Around fifteen metres to the right of the platforms facing from the lifts, there is a large raised rectangle control room built out from the wall overseeing the whole layout. There isn't much room inside, as it is filled with monitoring equipment. Either side of the control room is open storage – a dump area for miscellaneous tools, equipment and some boxes, nothing much to speak of. Opposite is a large sealed straight-walled room that is home to the power source, this is humming lightly, I would imagine for the replenishment of the air down here. Lying in front are the girders from the hoist. Overall, amazingly, the whole chamber is tidy and bright, not in a dilapidated state as expected so deep down.

'The scientists tell me that whatever was assembled down

here must be very big and the wide tracks mean heavy weight. The ample working space tells that story as well. The high dome means ample air supply for the whole complex what must be for dozens of workers. I presume they eat and slept down here.

'The four technicians are now in the crowded control room questioning the two Nacanians on the purpose of their last visit. The scientists, Dave and two guards are outside waiting on the balcony walkway and the stairs. Meanwhile the girl team has arrived, the last to come down until further instructions from Dave. Now making a total of twenty-seven in all down here. He then sent the personnel lift back to the upper cavern. Everybody is going about their business, not touching anything but checking out for any booby traps, inspecting the sealed door, and the power source – recording everything on cameras as evidence of the chamber and now managing to send TV pictures to the ship to show them the conditions the work force will be working under. The air is at last freshening.'

In the control room, a small fight started between one of the technicians and the two survivors. Outside, Dave and the two guards on the narrow balcony squeezed in to break it up and to find out the reason why.

'The two Nacanians are being difficult and awkward in explaining the controls in here. They are holding back information. I'm not taking the chance of turning off any switches until I am sure it is safe. It could be irreversible,' explained the technician. The others agreed with him. In fact, it turned out they were just plain scared and Dave calmed the situation down. The two admitted they did not know of the full workings of the complex. Their instructions were to switch that on and pull that, check that the go-ahead light was green before extinguishing itself, then check the system was in order

189

according to the manual instruction sheets. Then they said, make sure the clock is functioning with a verbal conformation as a final system check before going into silent automation.

'Now we are getting somewhere,' said one of the scientists on hearing the final sentence. 'Find that clock,' he ordered. Three of the technicians were left to take the whole of the control panel to bits, carefully avoiding any switches and suchlike where possible. Outside, everybody stood and waited. No further move could be made until this problem was solved.

An hour passed. The two scientists returned for a few minutes to confirm the report, then the control room was evacuated. The two scientists gathered everybody together along with the TV link to the mothership via the operations ship above, so that everyone could hear the news at the same time. 'There is a sealed box embedded in the floor under the control panels. It is timer countdown. The display shows just under twenty-nine hours to zero hour, that's 3 a.m. Monday Earth time. I am informed that any interference with any of its connecting system will set it to zero immediately. End of story, so my colleague and I will have to check what sort of device we are dealing with, and that is through that sealed tunnel door to see if we can do anything at that end. At the moment the prospects are not good at all.'

The six-man specialist team prepared to don environmental suits; they would use the flat carriage to travel through the tunnel to reconnoitre beyond the sealed door. The carriage was in working order and was placed up to the tunnel entrance. All was ready; one of the technicians was to drive while the others sat on boxes. Dave was in the control room with the Nacanians to press the appointed switch. Dan, Harry and Linda watched from the narrow control room balcony. Dave's girl team was watching from the control room steps. The remaining ten gathered in the vicinity of the lift shaft as a precaution. Dave pressed the switch and the power source

190

began to hum louder, and the door unsealed itself and slowly began to slide open.

For the next 90 seconds there was no live verbal record of what happened next, except blurred images on the monitor in the ship above and sound effects from Linda's recorder. Linda had to recall this section for the record much later:

'The tunnel door opened completely, allowing the carriage to enter into the unknown beyond. Then suddenly the Mother of all Hell broke loose. We were all watching the six-man team enter the tunnel when we saw eight concealed panels equally spaced high up around the domed wall slide back. Two of them were closer together above the tunnel, and they appeared to be monitoring cameras. They rotated and protruded quickly out from the recesses. They all zeroed onto the working platform area in front of the lifts. in a flash, beams of energy from all eight sprayed that area completely. Had there been a work force there, they all would have been eliminated in seconds.

I couldn't believe what I was witnessing, for a second it seemed I was on a James Bond film set. This illusion was soon dispensed with as I saw these weapons stop firing and start scanning menacingly like predictors looking for further life in the surrounding area. In that pause, Dave had dashed out from the control room, shouting to take cover and try to take out these weapons. The reality was that there was no cover to take. Very cleverly planned as these weapons covered every angle. That's why the girders were cut down for a free field of fire. Three of the girls with their light side-arms took out one of the weapons above and to the left behind us, between the lifts and the control room. Two of the men down by the lifts with their heavier weapons destroyed the one to their left opposite the control room, the others did the same to another two, one each side of the lifts. These two were placed lower, I presume to cover the tunnel entrance. From the unforeseen booby trap, these were the only four of the eight that were to be taken out, but this proved later to be a salvation. In split seconds these weapons now detected us at the opposite end to the tunnel entrance. I was told later that this slight delay saved most of us from death. The weapons were programmed to kill everybody on the platforms, had we gathered there to see the carriage move off on its journey, but luckily the carriage was moved up to the tunnel entrance and consequently saved the lives of the specialists. The opening of the tunnel door had apparently triggered the weapons.

With no cover available, Dave pushed the Nacanians to the the floor of the control room hoping the weapons sensors worked on the principle of heat and movement. As the weapons turned, the men exposed by the lifts made a desperate attempt to run zigzagging for the sanctuary of the tunnel. The remaining open-caged cargo lift offered no protection at all. Three diverted for the remaining railway carriage, to take cover underneath, protected at the sides from the raised railway platforms. They certainly didn't waste time in returning fire; these split seconds were vital. The rest perished before reaching the tunnel entrance. In this deadly commotion, Dave pulled Dan into the control room. Harry went to follow him holding my wrist as we dashed for the narrow steps to ground level, but there was no room, with the dismantled panels taking up most of the space. I was the last in the queue on the balcony; the girls had nowhere to go except into the dump area. We hadn't realised it, but it had become a part dead zone area from the remaining weapons angle of fire. The four weapons now turned on us; one of the girls was firing back from the dump, her shots going wild as the others bumped and scrambled past her. She took a full blast straight in the chest, another was wounded.

On my recorder later, I could hear the screams, especially mine, the shouting and the rapid "dert-dert" hollow sounds of these weapons reverberating – a sound I shall never forget.

192

At ground level, Harry turned around and pulled me in front of him. The noise was tremendous in the enclosed cavern. The firefight now engulfed us; all I could see were bright flashes of light passing around us in the smoke. The heat was building up. I saw one of the girls thrown through the air and crashed into the wall in the dump area. I was numb with fear; I didn't know which way to turn. There was an almighty bang behind us. I looked back, and Harry was shielding me from the blasts around us. We reached the dump and there was another salvo of blasts, this was the end as Harry held and covered me as he turned my body away as the splinter blasts from rock and concrete ricocheted all around us.

Suddenly both of us were thrown forcefully and heavily into the dump amongst the other girls taking the limited cover there. They used the body of one of their comrades along with the odd container boxes as partial shield cover. Suddenly all was quiet; we seemed to be out of shot of these murderous weapons. Harry was lying on top of me ... he was not moving. One of the girls shouted in the eerie silence. 'HARRY HAS BEEN HIT!' This part was clear on my recorder, and I also heard my reaction: 'OH GOD! NO!, PLEASE, HE CAN'T BE DEAD! ... Noooo.'

Harry was pulled off me and was dragged into the small tight triangle of the dead zone. His body was at our feet. This corner at the base of the control room was the only sanctuary we had. The six of us were squeezed into this tight corner.'

Nobody dared to move as the weapons sensors stopped picking us up. My body was shivering violently. I was on the verge of hysteria as I looked down at the body of Harry – I wanted to kneel down by him. The girls were restraining me.

Dan shouted to Dave, 'Turn the main power off.'

Dave got hold of the nearest Nacanian lying on the floor by him.

'Where is the main power switch?'

193

'No, you can't do that. It will set the timer to zero.'

'Then the power to the lights, for God's sake!'

'They are special camera weapons, they will still see you in the dark.'

'You ... yes, you,' stated Dave, he had a desperate idea as all hope faded. 'Dan. This room hasn't been hit. I think they are programmed to avoid it, and I'm taking a gamble the Nacanians have immunity from these weapons.'

'Christ, you are not going to ...'

'Yes I am. I've no choice.' Dave turned to the pair. He saw the fear in their eyes as they guessed his intentions. 'You two are going out there,' he stated, determined. He drew his weapon to show he meant business. Dave didn't like what he was forcing them to do – he didn't have any other option. 'And you will bring back,' continued Dave, 'four of my men's heavy weapons to me. Is that clear?'

Dave pressed his hand weapon between the eyes of the female and pushed. The pair backed off; slowly stood up and cautiously stepped out onto the balcony. Dan watched for reactions from the weapons outside. They moved and focused on the control room balcony, but they stayed silent.

'If I get out of this alive,' remarked Dan, 'I'm retiring. Kate mentioned it earlier.'

'About time, you lucky bastard,' replied Dave, smiling at him. 'About time you gave your wife some attention.' Both of them simultaneously in their strong friendship held out their hands and shook hard. They knew if this failed, death would be only minutes away. The remaining lift was still there, but no hope in hell of making it to the lift shaft, and communication with the surface was now completely down.

Dan shouted to the others their plans. They replied but they didn't tell him about Harry. Everybody waited as the pair slowly made their way down the steps. The moment of truth was about to be known.

12

The Nacanians were now in front of the control room; they walked slowly hand in hand towards the tunnel, only their eyes glancing up to the now deadly still weapons. They hadn't moved since the pair appeared on the balcony. 'So far so good,' said Dan to Dave, peering through the base of the window, 'Looks like your gamble has paid off.'

'I shall say yes to that when I'm walking down there,' replied Dave, not believing his lucky guess. 'I hope their programming hasn't a brain.'

Dave was thinking hard for other alternatives. He hoped this was not a Catch-22 situation, but so far this was the only option he had now clear in his mind. He couldn't take the chance on how they were programmed.

The three under cover of the remaining carriage kept well hidden as the tunnel weaponry cover them. They couldn't see or know what was going on above them. The five standing in the dead zone were waiting hopefully for the pair to return safely, their nerves on edge for the success or failure on their accomplishment. Linda was now squeezed tight into the corner for the team's charge to be reasonably safe, worked into there gradually by the girls. She could hardly breathe from being squashed, and the heat did not help. How long this would go on for, she had no idea. She closed her eyes and started to control her breathing and hopelessly tried to think of other things; this was impossible, with Harry's motionless body lying at her feet with a big hole in the back of his overalls.

The couple retrieved four weapons from the fallen and retraced their steps, as casually as possible. As they approached the steps, Dave crawled to the open door and instructed the two, as they reached the bottom step, to pass a weapon each butt first to the girls tight against the wall, one of whom would reach for it.

'Do you understand?'

'Yes, we do.'

'Did you hear that, girls?'

'Yes,' replied Ange. She sounded exhausted.

'Ah, Ange. Who is next to you?'

'Je ... Jen,' came Jen's hesitant nervous reply.

'You're doing a great job, girls, won't be long now,' said Dave, trying to boost their morale. Their first blood action initiation had taught them the hard way, in the deep end first in this noxious hellhole. Several minutes had now passed since the tunnel door opened and keeping everybody's mind occupied was very important, otherwise panic could eventually come into the equation.

The pair reached the steps and each successfully passed a weapon to Ange as she reached out, her back pressed tight against the side of the control room wall. The first one she passed on to Jen. Dave was relieved that there were no sudden explosions. The Nacanians were now back inside and passed the other two weapons to Dan. He told them to stay standing. Dave sat by the door, speaking quietly to his team, explaining his final plan of action. Finally he told them he was going to have to use an old cliché of distraction. He warned that it might or might not work, depending on how the Nacanian weapons were programmed 'Is there anything you can lob over this control room towards the tunnel?' he asked.

'No,' stated Ange. 'None of us can move let alone pick anything up.'

'Understood. Then I want you to lob your sidearms over instead,' instructed Dave compromising. 'In fact it's a better idea.'

'OK. I hope you know what you are doing,' replied Ange, curious.

'When I shout, Now, do it! When I shout, Now, for the second time, do as I have instructed. If you don't hear the second command, for your mother's sake don't move!' said Dave. 'Dan and myself are now going to test a theory first. Be ready.'

Dan and Dave checked their weapons, looked at each other and without saying a word stood up and made their way slowly onto the balcony and turned facing the tunnel, Dan was leading, very relieved he was still alive; the camera guns stayed silent.

It was about five short paces of hell to the end rail. 'Christ, Dave,' said Dan tight-lipped, as he took the first slow steps. 'Your weird theory is working. I feel I'm being lined up for the firing squad, and those bloody things are moving with us!'

'Shut up, Dan. We'll have a drink afterwards to celebrate.'

'You and your crazy ideas. Mine is a treble, and you're paying. I don't know how your girls put up with you.'

'Charisma, Dan. Pure charisma.'

Dan had to smile to himself. Dave was a good man, a cool mind even under this pressure. If he couldn't get us out of this bloody mess, then no one could.

Dan neared the end rail and stopped short of it, Dave close behind him.

'Ready?'

'As I ever will be.' Dan knelt down slowly and rested his weapon on the rail. He took aim in the general direction of his target. He had for the moment to keep his body back and in tight to the control room frontage, otherwise his intended target would be able to zero on to him, and that would not be good for his health. It was his choice to pick this one, as Dave was more experienced in the shooting department. Dan's target was to his right and only about eight metres away, at 45° up from him.

Dave stood behind him, concentrating on the four evil eyes clocking them. His target was to the right of the tunnel entrance, 25 metres distant. His second target, if the girls failed, was the one on the left of the tunnel, a longer shot of about 35 metres. The girls were at a disadvantage; they had to come out exposing themselves, and this would cost them seconds as well as taking aim. Their main target was opposite the control room, nearly 50 metres, and was the one pinning the girls down. Their second target was about 40 metres, was also Dave's second target; easy shooting when practising, but nerves, sweating and time to get in position added to the tension. Since stepping out from the door, about 30 seconds had ticked by – it seemed a lifetime.

'Are you ready, girls?' asked Dave. A hoarse reply reached him. 'Yes.'

'Charge those side-arms ...' pausing for a few seconds for them to heat up. 'NOW!' He aimed as four hand guns came lobbing over him and Dan. They bounced and slid on the concrete ahead of him, between the tunnel and the control room. YES! Dave saw in his field of vision, three of camera weapons zeroed in onto the handguns.

'NOW!' As loud as he could, Dan exposed himself and fired a split second after Dave just as the camera guns fired. Death came quickly for them as they blew to bits from the men's rapid fire. Dave swiftly turned to his second target. He lowered his weapon; there was no need. All he saw was a hole where his target was, and another big hole about 20 metres to the left of that. The two girls had done their job. He looked down and saw Ange and Jen and shouted, 'Well done girls.' They didn't hear his appraisal, for they were hugging each other and dancing up and down with elation. It looked like

Dave would have to eat his words on his joking remarks on the girls' erratic shooting on the practice range. On that he had no problem.

Linda was breathing heavily as she at last was able to kneel down to Harry, helped by the two other slightly wounded girls. His back was soaked in blood, and they turned him over. Linda felt for a pulse . . .

'Hello gorgeous . . . am . . . am I in heaven?' gasped Harry, wincing in pain while trying to smile.

Linda was taken aback in shock, she had thought the worst. Relieved and happy she embraced him hard, making him cry out in pain. 'Steady on, we are not in bed you know.'

'No, you sod,' smiling with tears running down her cheeks. 'All hell has now passed us by, thank God.'

'What happened?' he grimaced.

Linda explained briefly while the two girls cut the clothes off his back. The wound was about 15 centimetres long and down to the bone on his right shoulder blade. It looked as if someone had pressed a red-hot poker across the shoulder blade and held it there until it had burned to the bone. They guessed he had caught it on the turn as he pushed Linda down, otherwise he would have been hit square in the back. The girls treated him as best as they could with field dressings and injected him with a painkiller. In the anticlimax, Linda thought two of the girls were lost, but in the confusion she must have somehow seen the same girl twice.

Dave checked for casualties and injuries. Seven men down and three injured, plus sadly the eighth fatality was his latest member of his Close Protection Team, Cath, who had only been with them for a few weeks. He felt bitter with remorse, and responsible. Ange and Jen told him she fought like a veteran in her covering fire. The camera weapons had

199

zeroed on to the heat of her hand weapon, thus giving the others that edge to take cover.

Dave managed to re-establish contact with the ship and explained what happened. His instructions were to send the injured up and a clean-up squad would be sent down. His priority was the specialist party and their report. Linda was to stay with Dan. Dave was to go into the tunnel to see how the technicians had fared in finding the device if they hadn't returned within the next hour.

Harry stubbornly refused to go to the upper cavern. His place was by Linda's side and he was not coming this far, to be put to bed when he was within striking distance of what put him here in the first place. He classed himself as walking wounded. He asked the girls going up to say he'd be up on the next lift. Dave gave Harry his uniform jacket to put over his shoulders. Meanwhile the relief team arrived and saw the damage on the ground in and around the platforms and at the devastated area where the girls took refuge; there wasn't a mark on the control room.

Only two scientists returned within the allotted time and they were in a hurry. They had left the other four at the tunnel head to study and establish on which procedure was best. Surprisingly, they did not know of the carnage that went on a few seconds after they entered the tunnel. The scientists were in a hurry to have the workforce down as soon as possible because what they had found was big and too complicated to be made safe in the coming 29 hours.

The scientists reported their findings via the communications link to Voss: 'We have inspected the device; in fact they are two, defined into one. At the end of this tunnel there is a small cavern housing them. I had wondered why on this, now I know. We saw immediately what we are up against and I

200

want the workforce down here now with all the equipment, there's no time to lose.'

Voss ordered the workforce leader to get going. He had heard enough for the time being, and would receive all the gen when he arrived down there.

'Now for the real bad news,' continued the chief scientist. 'If and when this "bomb" detonates, it is the end of mankind on Earth. This is so powerful, England and half of France will be one big crater ten miles deep.' He had to stop there because everybody in earshot was struck dumb with shock, then all commotion broke loose. It took a while for him to continue. Voss remained silent then eventually as the noise died down said, 'Carry on, would you please.'

'Because the position of this site was nearly at the top of the world in relation to Earth's axis, the force and the power involved will knock the Earth off its axis completely and could possibly affect the spin and cause deviation of orbit as well. There will be no time for a nuclear winter, death would be timed in days rather than weeks or months as caused from a nuclear war ... back to the situation here, the two devices are facing each other, similar to a nuclear reactor layout. Separating them is a lead wall. This is well within the safety margins required to keep their influences apart.... Let me try to explain this more clearly. When you hold two magnets and bring them together you feel them repel against each other, the same with matter and anti-matter. You receive power from these elements. What we have here is two components not of this world, and they both come from separate planets. We used to mine them for power when combined together, although there's isn't any waste from them; we had to ban the use and the mining of them, as they are too unstable and volatile, nearly three thousand years ago. Going by what I have seen so far here and of the devices and the technology involved, these are at least two thousand five hundred years old!' Harry interrupted by cutting in strongly.

201

'Let me, or us for that matter, get this straight. This is how I understand what you are stating. You are saying this has been here for over two and half thousand years, sitting here through written history and before. Through forty reigns of Kings and Queens, plagues have passed, and a good thousand years of advancement, not to mention two world wars and in all the time we are sitting on a Doomsday bomb. That is some statement' I call it a revelation. Today is a DAY OF REVELATION!'

Linda checked her recorder, she had caught every word in the last few minutes, then the words sank in ... 'Ooh my God!' (Linda later edited Harry's statement and added the last sentence to emphasise the point.)

The scientist realised the significance of the statement he had just made and continued his explanation, a little slower this time. 'The explosive force of this "Doomsday" as you have aptly named it is the most ultimate powerful force in this galaxy. Take these two minerals and transmute them forcefully together, you will have the most violent reaction unimaginable barring the sun's energy. These two are designed to blow downwards and when the force can't go any further it will backlash on itself like a rubber ball rebounding off a wall, the velocity will be tremendous. If you four come with me I'll show you the layout while they are getting the equipment down, then please you must leave, I can't afford to have any dead wood down here getting in the way in the tunnels. I'm sorry.'

It took only a few minutes on the carriage to reach the end of the tunnel; there in the small domed area they saw where he had left the four technicians looking over a very complicated set-up. The senior technician came over to report on his further findings. His statement wasn't encouraging. The set-up was well-maintained and the computer link to the control room was fully operational, completely on-line, with surprisingly no faults to report. In other words, they could

202

not interfere in that department at all, in case they triggered off a safeguard or something. The only solution he could see in his survey was to dismantle the two devices ... in less than 29 hours!

Harry was shivering and beginning to feel groggy; shock reaction symptoms were now showing up from his wound. Dave ordered his party to return to the ship. They had seen what they wanted to see, and now they were in the way. At the lift shaft they had to wait for an empty returning lift in the hustle and bustle as men and equipment arrived and loaded onto the rail-track transporter carriages.

13

Sunday

The nurse wasn't very amused about having to wait for Harry to appear in the cargo hold, but seeing him in a state of shock brought out her true instincts in nursing. In the next 24 hours or so she guessed she would be kept busy with many various injuries from the men down below from the amount of equipment being handled around her. For the duration of this mission there was a doctor on board, and an emergency sick bay had been organised and set up in a corner of the now clearing cargo hold.

The doctor instructed the nurse, who gave Harry, now semi-conscious, a two-in-one injection for infection along with a sedative. What happened in the next few minutes astonished Linda. The nurse placed what appeared to be a sun lamp over Harry's right shoulder. The doctor put on a pair of glasses and started to adjust and focus the unseen light over the open wound, and within a minute Linda witnessed the wound healing as the damaged skin and muscle tissues regenerated slowly from the bone upwards and inwards as the wound closed.

'He'll be good as new when he wakes up, most of the shock should be gone by then. Just give him a quiet day to rejuvenate and rest his arm in a sling,' whispered the nurse to Linda.

Voss entered the hold ten minutes later wearing his white cloak of his Mastery position, to see how things are. He would have been down earlier, but consultations with the scientist in charge delayed him. He talked to Dan and Dave as Harry was taken to a crew cabin to sleep. Linda joined him after receiving a check-up and a sedative from the doctor. She found her clothes in the cabin and took off her borrowed cat suit, looked at it for a second and rolled it up.

In the morning, Linda awoke to complete silence in the latter half of the morning watch with everybody now resting. The ship had had to move to a quieter area as it was too near the town, away from the expected early-morning golfers. There was a guard outside their small cabin on Dave's instructions, who told her the ship was now waiting in an isolated field on the Oxford Plain waiting for news of any progress, as there had been a slow start in the cavern. This time, on hearing those latter words, her sleeping butterflies came aroused and they began to flutter.

Dave knocked and entered an hour later, first to see how Harry was doing. Linda asked was there any food to be had, as she realised they hadn't eaten since lunchtime yesterday. 'There are the ship's rations and most of that has gone down with the men,' Dave informed her. 'Don't worry, I've come to tell the three of you are going back to the *Lady Hamilton*, orders. There's no point in staying down here, and Harry has to return; you'll observe more in comfort from up there. There is a shuttle due here soon, with fresh food supplies. You will return on that.' He sounded as if he had other thoughts on his mind.

An hour later the shuttle arrived and docked in the hold to unload. Harry was up and walking, the nurse checked him over and put on an arm sling. Linda noticed she was very gentle with him and fussed unnecessarily with the sling. As they prepared to go, the ship had to manoeuvre sideways into an adjoining field, because a farmer decided to move his herd of cattle after milking to fresh pasture underneath them. Everybody watched in welcome amusement as the man and boy, oblivious of what was above them in the bright and clear early morning air, herded the mooing cows as they looked upwards in their hesitations.

Now clear, the shuttle left the loading bay with seven passengers on board, including the two wounded girls along with Ange and Jen, Dave had ordered them to return. Voss, he said, would be returning later in the day. All seven were looking forward to a hearty breakfast, and Linda hoped to reunite with Sarah.

Sarah had watched the reports yesterday from mid-evening when the mothership had lost radio contact. Only for a short while did the fuzzy pictures tell them they were in dire need of help. Sarah ended up in Kate's and Dan's quarters with Delia watching until well past midnight, relieved on seeing them return to the operations ship. Up early, Kate, Delia and Sarah met them emotionally at the docking bay while the other girls went off with their boyfriends.

With breakfast over, everyone felt a lot better, although very little was spoken in their contemplation as their thoughts were back in that cavern – no update on the progress below had reached them. Sarah would have told them if there had been, although eight hours had passed. Dan told them they would see their questions answered as he invited them to watch later from his quarters. Linda still had her butterflies and she knew perfectly well the real cause of them: Mum and Dad.

As they all made their way back to their respective quarters, Linda hung back chatting to Sarah, while Harry continued with the others. He looked back, but said nothing, he knew those two were becoming good friends. When they were out of sight, Linda confided with Sarah about her troubled thoughts. She told Sarah about her parents, and somehow thought it was wrong to ask Voss to save them compared with nearly six billion about to die. She felt she didn't have the right to ask. Sarah understood, but she couldn't give an answer – it was out of her jurisdiction. All she could do was to advise her to tell Harry at once; after all he was now her fiancé. If she didn't tell him he'd never forgive her. Linda thought on it for a few seconds and decided to wait; Harry was still a bit shocked to worry him further.

They caught up with the others. Harry said he was to shower then lie down for a while. 'I hope there is news soon ... are you joining me, Linda?' he said, inspecting his shoulder, not believing what he couldn't see in the mirror as she joined him in the shower. He thought the nurse had been kidding him along.

Sarah had broken her own rulebook concerning her duties about getting personally involved with people from Earth, Harry and Linda were an exception, and her instructions from the beginning were to look after them. She went immediately to speak to Dan in confidence. He listened and thanked Sarah; he will see Voss later, for he was now kicking himself for not thinking of her parents earlier. It was all on file!

At midday, Dan invited Linda and Harry around to watch the latest update reports. At this time the scientists were speaking, so it must be important with 15 hours to go. As the report came through, Linda switched on her recorder. She had been lazy this morning: while she had the chance while Harry was asleep, she should have brought herself up to date with her notes. Her last entry was Friday and today – she had a couldn't-care-less attitude. What with the stress and worry of Harry yesterday and now, today her parents, she was not in the mood for anything. Dan and Harry might have had their adventures over the last few years, she said to herself, but me, a mere office girl, a nonentity in comparison thrown suddenly uninitiated between these two inspiring men. She felt like Calamity Jane having a mid-life crisis.

The lead scientist began to speak, and Dan observed Linda.

'As you know, we have had a few problems, a very slow progression to start with. This was expected, and now we are slowly dismantling the two separate devices. The men down here have named them NAPOLEON and JOSEPHINE, working on the theme of "Not tonight, Josephine". Now to remind you what we are up against. Both of them are fifteen metres high, fifteen wide and twenty metres in length, and are embedded into concrete. They are joined together by a seal; this acts as a shield as well to keep the influences and their separate components apart. This we have discovered dissolves in the final minutes of the countdown. The computer controls this, so we can't touch it. Our choice, er ... I mean our only option, is to cut into the device and take it apart bit by bit. Josephine is the more volatile one from planet "X", and is encased in a protective jacket. All out efforts are working on that now. Napoleon, the key component of the two, is encased in metal containing the ten mineral rods from planet "Y" along with the chemical element that will react violently inside Josephine. Going by my calculations the rods must be at least fifteen metres long and over sixty centimetres in diameter. The rods are pushed into Josephine by rams enclosed in the rear of Napoleon; I have a small team investigating him. Individually, both are harmless to work on, but are very complicated in their complex state. We don't want to trip any wires with this computer ... we are using Lasers mainly to cut into them. Now I must get back, I'll give another update about six.'

'Well,' stated Harry, 'I hope we have a more encouraging report then. He wasn't very confident about the outcome, was he?'

Dan had closely observed Linda's reaction. She was hiding

it well, so far. But her eyes gave her away and also how she was stroking Susie on her lap. He was surprised Harry hadn't noticed, there again, he didn't know. It was time to put him wise.

He gestured to Harry and Kate that he wanted a quiet word. He told them they were going to the diner to bring back snacks; it was going to be a long day. Outside, he told them of Linda's concern. Kate had noticed with her experienced eye, but she was biding her time, now her suspicions were confirmed. Harry put it down to a mood or being over-tired. 'I had no idea,' he said shamefully. 'Linda has never mentioned her parents once since I have known her. I'm going to have a word with her now!'

'Carefully, Harry,' instructed Kate. 'Carefully, please.'

They followed Harry back and he went over to Linda. He said something to her. She looked up, smiled, nodded and placed Susie on the floor, stood up and followed Harry outside.

'We are going for a walk,' Linda said innocently and unperturbed.

Harry took her to the observation corridor, and for a change, it was nearly deserted. He walked slowly with her holding his left arm, with small talk he led her until the Earth came into view. This is the moment he thought, with Europe and Africa in full sunlight. Linda stopped, took in the sight, saw the UK at the top. Harry was silent, waiting. She felt his eyes on her as she realised, 14 hours to go. She looked up at him and he wasn't smiling. She knew he knew. The expected question came. Harry asked her three times. 'Have you something to tell me?' The third time her head was buried into his chest, his arms around her before she gave in, she had to answer him. For the next 20 minutes, he talked, consoled and saw she was the love of his life, and the fact that two people together do not hold secrets from each other. From his experience he did not want unnecessary unresolved tensions. Dan knew of the problem and would be seeing Voss on his return. 'Don't blame Sarah, as a concerned friend she took the right course of action, otherwise we wouldn't be out here.' With his good arm around her they eventually made their way back, Linda greatly relieved and her learning curves about men now complete.

On their return, snacks from the diner were laid out to help themselves. Dan was away at the Master's suite. Kate mentioned discreetly to Harry that she had sedatives if he needed them.

'Hopefully not, thank you. Will Dad be long?'

'I don't think so, he had that determined look in his eyes.'

At the Master's operations suite, only Eva and Lesley were in attendance as Dan entered. 'Any idea when Voss will be back?' Dan knew that when the boss was out the mice would play and the ladies would be more amenable and sociable. Understandable, but Dan knew them from years of experience. They had helped him a lot in the past. This time though, he sensed an atmosphere.

'He won't be,' replied Eva. 'He is staying down there to the bitter end. He is actually in the cavern watching the progress first-hand. This has been his life's work and vocation, to watch over Earth. He has warned us with code words that matters are not going well at all. He cannot leave until the end...'

'Oh. I see.' Dan swore she was going to add something to that last sentence. Like, 'if so, he will stay.' He continued, 'Well, I have a problem to sort out concerning our Linda, perhaps you could if possible, speak with Voss next time he calls.'

'Perhaps we can help,' replied Lesley. 'We do run his office, Dan, even in his absence. What is the problem?'

'I have slipped up,' confessed Dan, hiding his scruples. 'It concerns Linda's parents. Linda wants to know if she can bring them up here. It's my fault, I should have thought of it earlier.'

'I see the predicament,' stated Lesley. She turned to Eva with the question on her face. Eva nodded in their non-verbal exchange and then she spoke to Dan.

'We are telling you to wait until this evening, when we have the latest update. If it is for the worse, we let you know, then go and bring them here, you have our authority. We will sort out any problems later.' Her tone suggested Voss might not be returning. Lesley now spoke, 'I tell you now, all the operatives and their helpers have brought up their families, most of whom know, in case we failed and would have to start all over again. Voss received those orders from the Elders of the High Lords when the device was found. That order is classified until we know the outcome. They wish to speak with him personally, but he refuses to answer them; we had to cover for him.'

'Thank you,' replied Dan, shocked at those words. It was bad down there, that scientist was under orders not to reveal the truth until the eleventh hour. He looked at the security monitor that covered only Voss's movements. He saw a man sitting on a box in the cavern facing the tunnel wearing a black cloak, his head covered by the hood, not his usual white one with the hood down.

He left the operations suite quickly; he couldn't stay in there any longer, knowing the truth. All he had in his thoughts now was, do I tell the others...?

A few minutes later Dan returned to his quarters. On the way he decided to tell the truth, but not to Linda until the outcome was known. He whispered a few words to Kate, nodded to Harry sitting by Linda, her eyes closed, resting. Harry casually stood up and came over to them. In Kate's small kitchen Dan explained the truth, that they were to go tonight if Eva and Lesley heard the code word for the worse. Harry agreed not to reveal the whole truth to Linda. He returned and sat by Linda, now in conversation with Delia. Smiling, he simply told her the good news that Voss had given permission and they would go tonight if the situation didn't improve. Linda was relieved her conundrum was now in good hands.

For the rest of the afternoon everyone patiently waited, sometimes impatiently, for the promised update at six. Harry took Linda for a stroll to break the tedium of time; also Linda wanted to see Sarah to apologise and thank her. After enquiries they found her off-duty in her room, listening to the odd activity in the cavern like everybody else in the ship. The only live pictures on the monitor were restricted to the tunnel entrance. Sarah welcomed them and for an hour chatted until her boyfriend turned up at the end of his duty.

At six, nearly every monitor on the *Lady Hamilton* went blank. Except for a few essential personnel, the ship's complement switched to the transmission channel from Earth. The screens were blank for nearly ten minutes as the crew waited. All activity in and outside the ship had ceased. The Captain had the foreknowledge of the crew's reaction and accordingly had taken steps for security and safety for the forthcoming hours.

In the Log he said: 'In my entire career I have never experienced a dead ship, yet there are thousands on board. It is still, no movement at all. In or out. Only one child is in operation from this mothership, and that is down on Earth waiting like the rest of us, hoping that tomorrow we are still employed in our life's work. If we fail in our task, I have before me sealed orders addressed to myself, the Captain, and the Master. On the bridge with me are three of the

Elders of the High Lords who have arrived this afternoon to oversee the situation, but mainly to observe first-hand. I do know, and dread, what my first command would be, to go in on close orbit around Earth. I also know that the *Lord Nelson* and her consort along with our replacement are on full emergency light travel to our aid.' End of Log report. Sun, 17.30hrs, 01.07.01. Ship Earth time.'

At ten past six, the screens came alive and the scientist apologised for the delay; he had to give his report to Voss first. With the tunnel entrance in the background he began to speak: 'First of all I have good and some bad news. The bad news is that we had to abandon Josephine. She is proving to be too complicated in the time available, as I predicted. The small team I had on Napoleon has found an Achilles heel in the ramrods department. We have gained excess by cutting away the outer cover at the rear and at this moment we are dismantling the pistons. I must add, the mechanisms are not being touched or any of the wiring so this doesn't leave us much room to work in, but the door is open for us to make headway. Because of the confined space the heat in the small cavern is now 120 degrees and rising from the cutting lasers. I have called for fans and air conducting and conditioning generators, and my men are now working in half-hour shifts. If I can remove the threat of Napoleon, then we have won. To do that I have to remove the chemical mineral rods from inside the tubes that line up with Josephine. The make-up of these rods is similar to aluminium, so they are easy to cut. The problem is time, because in the limited space at the rear we have to cut the rods into two-metre sections as we withdraw them. There are ten rods, and each one is fifteen metres in length. Complete removal of the rods is essential if we don't want Josephine to mate tonight, and the safest distance is in the large cavern. I will give a progress update at nine, hopefully sooner. Our deadline down here at this moment in time is two a.m ... thank you.'

As the carriage he arrived on returned to the tunnel, the camera zoomed back a little, and very briefly a shoulder cloaked in black appeared and the side of a man's face showed. Those very few in the know knew it was the Master and his hood was down ... there was hope yet!

About three hours wait for more news and eight for the stated deadline was like watching paint dry, when out of the blue it was announced that live coverage had been granted. Where it could be heard there were loud cheers. Apparently the three Elders had stepped in and overruled the previous order. Now everybody could watch, and even those on duty had a monitor near by.

In Dan's quarters they watched and waited as the cameras were set up out of the way and not too close. At least there were live pictures now and this made a huge difference in the psychology of a waiting audience.

Over an hour later, the transporter carriage emerged from the tunnel with eight parts on board from the first withdrawn rod from Napoleon. They went straight into the lift to the upper chamber. Harry was impressed at watching these men rotating in teams as they cursed and sweated in the restricted space. One or two men did collapse or were injured before the second rod was removed around eight p.m., and each time another man was waiting to step forward to take his place. Soon breathing apparatus had to be worn at all times, and the rotating relief teams were taking shorter breaks. Harry had the impression that this race of people are all $E=MC^2$ and had gone passive with their automation technology. Not these men, even the specialist team who are in the front end of it all, were helping, advising, watching, warning of slip-ups for danger, and for longer periods overall. At this rate it took no mathematician to work out that time would win this race.

This time when the carrier came out of the tunnel, the scientist was on board for the update, earlier than expected. With him was the engineering technician, to back up his next move. Voss didn't intervene on this occasion; he must have gestured them to go straight up to the camera team, knowing the Elders were on board the mothership and because time and effort was entirely in their hands now. Breathlessly, his words were brief this time:

'We think we have mastered the solution now. We had to proceed with caution on the first one. Now the clock is against us. If Dave would release me his men to operate the transporter carriages and take the cut parts of Napoleon up to the upper cavern, that will give me more men to use as a extra team to withdraw and cut two rods at the same time, thus halving our time. Now I must return.' Dave must have received the nod, for he gathered his men on the carriage and disappeared into the tunnel.

Between then and midnight, Dave's security men brought six rods to the cavern. He had split his men into three teams, one to the carriages, another to load the lift and the third to unload at the upper chamber. Nobody travelled in the lifts, except once for the doctor escorted by Dave to administer injections to the resting men. Food and plenty of refreshments were loaded on the return journeys. From the upper chamber the ship's crew beamed the rods to the ship's cargo hold. This extra help gave the salvage men more breaks in the rotating system and fewer accidents to contend with.

Monday

Dan hadn't received the expected code word from the ladies in Voss's suite. Seeing Linda looking to him apprehensively since the eighth rod had arrived in the cavern, he reassured her that he thought there would be no need to collect her parents; either way there was still plenty of time, but he would check just in case. As before, he didn't use the ship's computer personal visual contact network in case there was a problem and the prospect of Linda overhearing him. He could go private, but Linda was too near and she would wonder why. He waited for a few more minutes, then he saw the first segments of number nine emerge from the tunnel. He looked at his watch; hmmm ... we will wait a little longer.

From Linda's point of view, her trust in Dan was implicit. For the last few hours she was relaxed in the knowledge that Mum and Dad would be saved. In the back of her mind she knew that if her parents were rescued prematurely and this proved to be unnecessary (on this point she felt cruel and hard), this would create problems for her in the future. For one, Mum could not keep a secret. Two, the media and security and above all their safety, and of course herself. Three, Linda had no wish for her parents to know whatsoever, as she planned to be incognito as long as possible, depending on the long-term political situation of the future. If it went pear-shaped in the next two hours, then all the above would clearly be irrelevant.

With one and a half hours to go on the countdown, a call came through on Dan's personal inner ear communicator from Lesley. He coughed then listened nonchalantly to the news coming through to him. With these things no one else could hear the messages so he patiently waited for Lesley to finish. Kate was watching him closely, and she knew when he coughed again. The times she had heard those little coughs in the past when he was summoned. His eyes smiled at her knowing stare.

Before he could open his mouth to speak, Kate spoke out. 'Well?' she said, getting up from her seat and walking over to him, 'What is happening?' The other three looked at Dan, realising he had received news.

'What have you heard?' finished Kate; her words hung in the air as everybody stood up and questionably faced him.

'All is well!' he stated happily and relieved. 'All is well. Number nine, we gathered, was a bitch and number ten is being removed now, and in another half an hour or so, all will be clear.' In seconds the solemn atmosphere changed dramatically to relief with joy and elation as the weight of worry and the tension lifted off their shoulders.

By 2.45 every man down below was back in the operations ship, where many were being treated mainly for minor injuries, exhaustion and dehydration. Many just fell asleep as they sat down and relaxed. For the record, all the cameras were set up to witness the final countdown procedure.

At 3 a.m. precisely, the hydromechanics behind the ram-rods activated and Napoleon went through the motions of pushing the now non-existent rods into the tubes of Josephine. The combined seal and shield that separated them a few seconds earlier now dissolved into a jellied gunge on the floor. Everything worked according to plan on the antiquated well-maintained set-up that gave a highly advanced race a run for its money.

Two minutes later, if it hadn't been for Dan's map and Harry's educated and spot-on guess. Plus the infinite technology know-how from start to finish with men whom Harry, mistakenly but now very impressed overall, had thought earlier were from a meek civilised race contributing from living a long automated age. Then down into the harsh Stone Age conditions, along with one very lucky fluke with a pro-grammed booby-trap that did cause casualties, which would've wiped out all their former efforts. Earth would now be in its dying throes of extinction.

Now everything was dead and safe below. The program-ming had run its course. Later the decision would be made to leave Josephine where she lay, now completely harmless, to be buried for all time. This was done by destroying the control room, wrecking the power source opposite, then as they retreated from Josephine, releasing pressurised foam which expanded and filled the void from the cavern, along the tunnel to the main cavern. Two men at the lifts observed the expansion creeping towards them as they released further foam canisters before leaving to the surface, the lifts powered from the ship directly overhead. The same process was applied to the lift shafts and the upper cavern. In a few hours the foam was hard as rock, filling every nook and cranny.

In the survey examination conducted before destroying the complex, the findings stated that the small upper cavern was originally on the surface in a hollow of the surrounding land. When completed, a domed roof was built over the lift shafts and covered over from the waste material from the excavations and landscaped. All this had been done about a thousand years before the Nacanians were politically policed in their determination to be completely separate in their premeditated hostile policy of independence.

Tuesday and Wednesday

Now that the threat of extinction was removed, the planned Peace and Environmental Conference of the world's leaders could proceed. By early Monday evening, *Lady Hamilton* was ready to receive her VIP guests. The salvage team had returned home in triumph earlier that day.

Now nearing midnight above the longitude of the United States Eastern Sea Board and with Europe asleep, every available shuttle of all types left the mothership for Earth followed closely by the freighters to rendezvous with the smaller vessels after they had abducted all the premiers from about 170 nations around the world. Accompanying every President, Prime Minister, Dictator, Head of State and Royalty were one, two or three important Government

218

officials to witness and attend the conference – in the case of the US President, at least five, including his speech writer/prompter . . . to start with, Zero Tolerance was displayed until they all realised what was happening to them and informed on the reasons why. They observed their journey to the stars, via one complete orbit of their home world.

On their arrival, representatives looked after each delegation with the liberty of freedom of speech to answer all questions concerning the P and E Conference, and full hospitality was shown and given. A short guided tour was allowed late Tuesday morning with a preliminary lecture start of the world's P and E Conference in the afternoon, followed by an informal gathering in the evening. Wednesday was Conference day commencing a 8 a.m. and held before all the 24 Elders of the High Lords. Questions were asked and the answers debated, after the requirements requested explained on Earth's peace and environmental future.

During Monday, Harry (now cleared with a clean bill of health) and Linda were briefed on the Conference. Linda in the afternoon caught up with most of her notes with Harry and Dan's help, mainly on the technical points. Outstanding statements would be forthcoming. Late evening from the observation corridor they watched dozens of ships stream in line, destination Earth.

Tuesday they kept out of the way, tuning in to watch the news reports from Earth. As expected, nothing was mentioned of the 'missing' Heads of State from all around the world. Both of them could imagine the chaos going on behind closed doors; but this was another story. Each Government in turn had time to cover the mystery disappearances and so discovering this had happened in all the nations worldwide, would have put out a global news blackout. Later in the afternoon the leaders attended the lecture. There they saw four people arrive to sit to the rear of the Elders and on full view the whole delegation. When the young couple arrived and sat down with Voss and Dan in their white cloaks on either side of them, the Conference room hushed but nobody stood up to question to whom they were.

On Wednesday, the question did arise, as their curiosity got the better of them. This was one question in the duration the representatives were not allowed to reveal. At 8.05 a.m., one appointed man stood up and enquired of the Elders, 'Who are those three people behind you? They are not from your race. In fact they look as if they are from ours.'

The middle Elder, the speaker for the High Lords, rose to his feet lowered his hood and turned to the three behind him to stand up. This was totally unexpected: Linda grasped the hands of Harry and Dan either side of her. She felt the reassuring squeeze from each of them as she faced nearly 500 people before her. Standing between her two men, Linda stood tall and proud from the privilege honoured her.

The Elder spoke. As he did so the other 23 Elders all dressed in their red cloaks turned in their seats and faced the nervous three, dropping their hoods in respect.

'The three you see ... are from Earth, from the country of England. They have been especially chosen by us for their role in this matter of leading up to this World Conference. The man on your left has been with us for over thirty years, and the younger man is his son, who has become involved in the last month. Up to then, his father was classified as missing. Our dear young lady is a writer and a correspondent, and she also has been with us a month and, I like to add, is now engaged to the man on her left. These two men are experts in geology and understand our concern of the Earth's environmental issues. Our young lady has been commissioned by us to write her official report from her prospective to join alongside our assessment of the official findings. She also has the prerogative to write her own personal story of her experiences in the last four weeks. Our permission for her publication will be granted at sometime in the future.

That is all you need to know ... Now let us proceed with the conference.'

To the hushed audience, this meant there was an outsider to their Government circles, who knew more than they did and was connected to the media as well.

It was a long day. The meeting came to an end mid-evening and the whole delegation returned home that night.

Time would tell if the world was to change. Future meetings were planned in the coming months. The main theme was that every government was in agreement from this initial important meeting to start the process of reviving Earth to her former glory of health, before it was too late, from the slow environmental stranglehold gathering momentum.

Linda took it for granted up to now, but over the two days she discovered two things. Attending the Conference, she understood every question, whether it was in Russian, Chinese or Mohican for that matter. She asked Sarah about it on how it worked. Sarah replied that she didn't know how the translation works, and even if she did it would be too complicated to explain. Then she stated, 'I just answered you in English, now I'm talking to you in my own language. Just accept our technology as you accept yours on Earth.' Linda looked at her surprised and replied, 'Well, I couldn't tell the difference in your speech at all. Amazing!' Then with a straight face she said, 'If I talk gobbledegook ... would you understand me?'

'Don't push your luck,' stated Sarah, seeing the joke. 'I just might, and put you in a home.'

The second thing Linda discovered was that she was not getting her normal advance body feelings that happened every month. This told her if she is in for a quiet or rough time. This time, out of pure curiosity about medical science here, she went for a check-up. When she left the ship's doctor, Linda had a smiling shocked expression on her face. They could tell so early that she was now pregnant. Later, with a sort of dazed innocent look that Harry wouldn't be able to read, she intended to surprise him, happily, so soon after his wicked ways with her.

My odyssey now ends.

EPILOGUE

At the weekend Delia, Harry and I arrived home for good. Our feelings on our return as we looked around were, what would've been, could've been. My commission was now completed with help from the ship's resources. Dan announced that he would retire by the end of the year, to resettle on Earth with Kate. Harry offered him half the house his father loved. Dan gladly accepted with our blessings. We thought he was joking, and this proved to be non-vexatious when he stated he would like to repair and convert the barn garage to 'park' his beloved Wanderer...

Delia stayed on in service, which I benefited from – I learned to cook – and as a part-time nanny. Harry and I were married three months later in a small private ceremony, with Sarah, Voss and Dave as special guests. Consequently, this enabled me to delay Harry's departure to the States that month. Six months later, I asked Sarah to be godmother to our two baby daughters. I thought it most appropriate. While I was carrying, I prepared all my notes and disc recordings to write this personal account. I completed a rough MS before I gave birth and left it like that for a couple of years. I knew the permission to publish would be some time coming.

Voss is still the Master in the mothership with the same crew. He won't retire!

Of the two Nacanian survivors? The Elders resettled them to colonise the next available planet with help from volunteers. The *Lady Hamilton* is to be recommissioned from cannibalisation for this sole purpose. The spy theory was never proven. Voss believes it stems from a temporary security misdemeanour in code reading that is all he would reveal.

Although we remained incognito, Harry still carried on with his vocation. Dan informed me not to worry over this, as we are being looked after. This brings me to my last words in this book.

In time, rumours and stories leaked out within the media about the mysterious young Earth woman reporter at the conference. Some reporters tried to trace me, but reaching an early dead end, they gave up, except for one, whose persistence I admired, because I knew him. He came close to finding my identity, but he found unexplainable little things happening to him in his quest that told him he was being gently warned off. His intuitions gave him his answer on how close he was in finding me, and sensibly he held back biding his time and his secret. I am certain he knew who I was.

I typed him a letter keeping my anonymity when I heard of this, and mailed the letter in London to him via his office. I explained briefly in one paragraph that I knew of his intentions, and if he was patient, then one day, when the New World settles down, he would have my exclusive life story.